PENGUIN BOOKS

EUGENE ONEGIN

Alexander Sergeyevich Pushkin was born in Moscow in 1799. He was liberally educated and left school in 1817. Given a sinecure in the Foreign Office, he spent three dissipated years in St Petersburg, writing light, erotic and highly polished verse. He flirted with several pre-Decembrist societies, composing the mildly revolutionary verses that led to his disgrace and exile in 1820. After a stay in the Caucasus and the Crimea, he went to Bessarabia, where he wrote *The Prisoner of the Caucasus* and *The Fountain of Bakhchisarai*. His work took a more serious turn during the last year of his southern exile, when he began *The Gipsies* and *Eugene Onegin*. In 1824 he moved to his parents' estate at Mikhaylovskoye in north-west Russia and spent two fruitful years, during which he wrote his great historical drama *Boris Godunov*, continued *Eugene Onegin* and finished *The Gipsies*. With the failure of the Decembrists' rising in 1825 and the succession of a new tsar, Pushkin recovered his freedom. During the next three years he wandered restlessly between St Petersburg and Moscow. He wrote *Poltava*, an epic poem, but little else. In 1829 he went with the Russian army to Transcaucasia, and the following year he retired to a family estate at Boldino, completing *Eugene Onegin*. In the autumn of 1830 he wrote *Tales of Belkin*, and his experimental 'Little Tragedies' in blank verse. In 1831 he married the beautiful Natalia Goncharova. The rest of his life was plagued by debts and the malice of his enemies. His literary output slackened, but he wrote two prose works, *The Captain's Daughter* and *The Queen of Spades*, and several folk poems, including *The Golden Cockerel*. Towards the end of 1836 anonymous letters goaded Pushkin into challenging a troublesome admirer of his wife to a duel. Pushkin was mortally wounded and died in January 1837.

ALEXANDER PUSHKIN

Eugene Onegin

A NOVEL IN VERSE

Translated by Babette Deutsch

PENGUIN BOOKS

PENGUIN BOOKS

Published by the Penguin Group
Penguin Books Ltd, 27 Wrights Lane, London w8 5tz, England
Penguin Putnam Inc., 375 Hudson Street, New York, New York 10014, USA
Penguin Books Australia Ltd, Ringwood, Victoria, Australia
Penguin Books Canada Ltd, 10 Alcorn Avenue, Toronto, Ontario, Canada m4v 3b2
Penguin Books (NZ) Ltd, Private Bag 102902, NSMC, Auckland, New Zealand

Penguin Books Ltd, Registered Offices: Harmondsworth, Middlesex, England

This translation first published 1964
1 3 5 7 9 10 8 6 4 2

This translation of Eugene Onegin *is based on that contained in* The Works of Alexander
Pushkin, *selected and edited, with an Introduction, by Avrahm Yarmolinsky (Random House,
1936), and is published by arrangement with Random House. By permission of Ginn & Co., hereby
gratefully acknowledged, in the present edition use has been made of certain passages from* Eugene
Onegin *in a version that appeared in* The Heritage of European Literature, *Volume Two (Ginn
& Co., 1949). Further revisions have been made in the text and a translation has been added of
'Excerpts from Onegin's Travels' and the extant fragments of Chapter Ten, two items not
available in the Random House* Eugene Onegin.

Printed in England by Clays Ltd, St Ives plc

Eugene Onegin

A NOVEL IN VERSE

Pétri de vanité il avait encore plus de cette espèce d'orgueil qui fait avouer avec la même indifférence les bonnes comme les mauvaises actions, suite d'un sentiment de supériorité, peut-être imaginaire.

TIRÉ D'UNE LETTRE PARTICULIÈRE

DEDICATION

Not with a notion of delighting
Proud worldlings, but to pleasure you,
For friendship's sake would I were writing
A nobler page, more fine and true,
Worthy of him I am addressing,
Whose days are living poetry –
Affection's pledge, indeed, expressing
Your dreams, your high simplicity.
No matter – ah, but look with favour
Upon the chapters in your hand,
Half-grave, half-gay, and with a flavour
Of what is common, what is grand;
To this were fribbling hours devoted,
Late nights, yes, and a facile art;
Fruit of spoiled years, or green and tart,
The mind's reflections coldly noted,
The bitter insights of the heart.

CHAPTER ONE

Makes haste to live and cannot wait to feel.
PRINCE VYAZEMSKY

I

'My uncle always was respected,
  But his grave illness, I confess,
  Is more than could have been expected:
  A stroke of genius, nothing less!
He offers all a fine example.
But, God, such boredom who would sample
As day and night to have to sit
Beside a sick-bed – think of it!
Low cunning must assist devotion
To one who is but half-alive;
You puff his pillow and contrive
Amusement while you mix his potion;
You sigh and think with furrowed brow:
"Why can't the devil take you now?"'

'Tis thus the gay dog's thoughts are freighted,
As through the dust his horses fare,
Who by the high gods' will is fated
To be his relative's sole heir.
Friends of Ruslan and fair Ludmila,
For my new hero prithee feel a
Like kinship, as he takes his bow;
Become acquainted with him now:
Eugene Onegin, born and nourished
Where old Neva's grey waters flow,
Where you were born or as a beau,
It may be, in your glory flourished,
I, too, strolled there – not recently:
The north does not agree with me.

3

A man of rank, his worthy father
Would always give three balls a year;
He lived in debt, and did not bother
To keep his hopeless ledgers clear.
Fate guarded Eugene, our young waster;
While in due time *Monsieur* replaced her,
At first *Madame* controlled the child;
The charming lad was rather wild.
Monsieur l'Abbé, a Frenchman, seedy,
Thought sermons fashioned to annoy;
He spared the rod to spoil the boy,
And in a voice polite but reedy
Would chide him, would forgive him soon,
And walk him in the afternoon.

When Eugene reached the restless season
Of seething hopes and giddy play,
And melancholy minus reason,
Monsieur was sent upon his way.
Now my Onegin, keen as brandy,
Went forth, in dress – a London dandy,
His hair cut in the latest mode;
He dined, he danced, he fenced, he rode.
In French he could converse politely,
As well as write; and how he bowed!
In the mazurka, 'twas allowed,
No partner ever was so sprightly.
What more is asked? The world is warm
In praise of so much wit and charm.

Since but a random education
Is all they give us as a rule,
With us to miss a reputation
For learning takes an utter fool.
Onegin, wiseacres aplenty
Called learned, although not yet twenty
And some harsh judges found, forsooth,
A very pedant in the youth.
A gifted talker, he could chatter
With easy grace of this and that,
But silent as a sage he sat
When they discussed some weighty matter,
And with the spark of a *bon mot*
He set the ladies' eyes aglow.

As Latin's held not worth attention,
His knowledge of the tongue was slight:
Of Juvenal he could make mention,
Decipher epigraphs at sight,
Quote Virgil, not a long selection,
And always needing some correction,
And in a letter to a friend
Place a proud *vale* at the end.
He had no itch to dig for glories
Among time's ruins, thought it just
That dusty annals turn to dust,
But knew the most amusing stories
That have come down the years to us
Since the dead days of Romulus.

The art of verse, that lofty pleasure,
He scorned, our Eugene never knew
Trochaic from iambic measure,
In spite of all we tried to do.
Theocritus and Homer bored him;
If true delight you would afford him
You'd give him Adam Smith to read.
A deep economist, indeed,
He talked about the wealth of nations;
The state relied, his friends were told,
Upon its staples, not on gold –
This subject filled his conversations.
His father listened, frowned, and groaned,
And mortgaged all the land he owned.

His wealth of skills is past relating,
But for one thing he had a bent,
And I am not exaggerating
His principal accomplishment.
From early youth his dedication
Was to a single occupation;
He knew one torment, one delight
Through empty day and idle night:
The science of the tender passion
That Ovid sang, that brought him here,
And closed his turbulent career
In such a miserable fashion –
Ovid, who found, so far from Rome,
In these bare steppes an exile's home.

9–10*

He early played the gay deceiver,
Concealed fond hopes, feigned jealousy,
With glib words won the unbeliever,
Seemed sunk in gloom, or bold and free,
Would turn quite taciturn with languor,
Then flash with pride and flame with anger,
Show rapture or indifference,
Or burn with sudden eloquence!
The letters that he wrote so neatly,
So easily, with passion seethed.
One thing alone he loved, he breathed;
He could forget himself completely.
His eyes, how tender, quick and clear,
Or shining with the summoned tear!

11

He knew the ruses that would brighten
The eyes of the ingenuous young;
He could pretend despair, to frighten,
Or use the adulator's tongue;
He'd catch the moment of emotion,
And out of an old-fashioned notion,
The strait-laced innocent beguile
With skill and passion, touch and smile.
He would implore the shy confession,
Catch the first stirrings of the heart,
Secure a tryst with tender art,
And at the following sweet session
Would, *tête à tête*, where no one heard,
Instruct the fair without a word.

12

In no time he learned how to flutter
The heart of the confirmed coquette!
What biting words the rogue would utter
Of those he wished her to forget!
None was so quick as he at trapping
A rival, or to catch him napping.
You men who lived in wedded bliss
Remained his friends, I grant you this.
The shy spouse whom Faublas had taught, he
Would find the soul of friendliness;
Suspicious age could do no less,
Nor yet the cuckold, stout and haughty,
Whose satisfactions were, through life,
Himself, his dinner, and his wife.

After an evening's dissipations
He will lie late, and on his tray
Find notes piled high. What? Invitations?
Three ladies mention a soirée,
Here is a ball, and there a party;
His appetite for pleasure's hearty –
Where will my naughty lad first call?
Tut! He'll find time for one and all.
Meanwhile, in morning costume, gaily
Donning his wide-brimmed Bolivar,
He joins the throng on the *boulevard*,
To promenade, as all do daily,
Until Breguet's unsleeping chime
Announces it is dinner-time.

16

At dusk a sleigh's the thing, and calling:
'Make way! Make way!' along they fly.
Upon his beaver collar falling,
Like silver dust the snowflakes lie.
Talon's his goal, no hesitating:
His friend [Kaverin] must be waiting.
He comes: a cork pops, up it goes,
The vintage of the comet flows.
A bleeding *roastbeef*'s on the table,
And truffles, luxury of youth,
French dishes for the gourmet's tooth,
And Strasbourg pies, imperishable;
Here's every dainty that you please:
Gold pines, and live Limburger cheese.

Glass after glass is drained in drenching
The hot fat cutlets; you would say
They've raised a thirst there is no quenching.
But now it's time for the ballet.
The theatre's wicked legislator,
Who unto every fascinator
In turn his fickle flattery brings,
And boasts the freedom of the wings,
Onegin flies to taste the blisses
And breathe the free air of the stage,
To praise the dancer now the rage,
Or greet a luckless Phèdre with hisses,
Or call the actress he preferred
Just for the sake of being heard.

Oh, land of boundless fascination!
There bold Fonvizin, freedom's friend,
Sped shafts of satire at the nation,
Knyazhnin played ape there without end,
Semyonova there wrought her magic
With Ozerov's grave lines and tragic.
Katenin at a later day
Revived the grandeur of Corneille;
There Shakhovskoy brought noisy laughter
With his sardonic comedies;
Didelot enjoyed his victories
Upon those very boards thereafter.
Where, in the shadow of the wings,
My youth fled by, remembrance clings.

My goddesses! How shall I trace you?
I sadly call on each sweet name.
Can others ever quite replace you?
And you, can you remain the same?
Oh, once again will you be singing
For me? Shall I yet see you winging
Your way in soulful flight and free,
My fair Russian Terpsichore?
Or must I with dull glances follow
Strange faces mid the painted set,
And having stared through my lorgnette
At the gay spectacle turned hollow,
Observe it with a yawn at last,
And silently recall the past?

The theatre's full, the boxes glitter,
The stalls are seething, the pit roars,
The gallery claps and stamps, a-twitter;
The curtain rustles as it soars;
A fairy light about her playing,
The magic of the bow obeying,
A crowd of nymphs around her – lo!
Istomina on lifted toe.
One foot upon the floor is planted,
The other slowly circles, thus,
Then wafted as by Eolus
She flies, a thing of down, enchanted;
Now serpentine she twists and wheels,
And now she leaps and claps her heels.

The house rocks with applause; undaunted,
And treading toes, between the chairs
Onegin presses; with his vaunted
Aplomb, he lifts his eye-glass, stares
Askance at fair, unwonted faces,
Remarks the jewels and the laces,
And notes complexions, with a sneer
Briefly surveying every tier,
He bows to sundry friends; his mocking
Slow eyes come last to rest upon
The lighted stage, and with a yawn
He sighs: 'They're past the age – it's shocking!
I've haunted the ballet – what for?
Even Didelot becomes a bore.'

The imps and cupids, quick as monkeys,
Upon the boards still flutter free,
While in the lobby sleepy flunkeys
Are guarding fur-coats faithfully;
Within, you hear the feet still pounding,
The coughs, the shouts and hisses sounding.
The noses blown, and without pause,
Above it all, the wild applause.
The carriage horses, chilled with waiting,
Impatient, twitch beneath the lamp,
The coachmen round the bonfires tramp,
Their masters wearily berating.
But our Onegin's out of range
Of curses: he's gone home to change.

23

Shall I depict less with a prudent
Than with a wholly faithful pen
The cabinet where fashion's student
Is dressed, undressed and dressed again?
All that the London fashions hallow
And that for timber and for tallow
Is shipped across the Baltic Sea
To please capricious luxury,
And all that Paris, mercenary
As she is modish, can devise
By way of costly merchandise
To tempt the gay voluptuary,
Whatever imports are the rage
Adorn the cell of our young sage.

24

Here's bronze and china in profusion,
And Turkish pipes of amber rare,
And, for the senses' sweet confusion,
Perfumes in crystal cut with care;
Steel files and combs of various guises,
And brushes, thirty shapes and sizes,
That teeth and nails may both be served,
Are here, with scissors straight and curved.
Rousseau (forgive me if I chatter)
Could not conceive how pompous Grimm
Dared clean his nails in front of him –
The fluent madcap! – but no matter:
In this case it is not too strong
To call that friend of freedom wrong.

A man of sense, I am conceding,
Can pay attention to his nails;
Why should one quarrel with good breeding?
With some folk, custom's rule prevails.
My Eugene was Chadayev second:
With every jealous word he reckoned,
He was a pedant, nothing less,
In the particulars of dress.
To prink and preen he'd need no urging,
But spend three hours before the glass,
Till from his dressing-room he'd pass
Like Aphrodite thence emerging,
Did giddy deity desire
To masquerade in male attire.

Now having given due attention
To a *toilette* you must admire,
The learned world would have me mention
Each detail of our friend's attire.
One takes a risk in such discussion,
Because there are no words in Russian
For *trousers*, *dress-coat*, and for *vest*;
But then, it puts me to the test,
For as it is, my style is peppered
With foreign words; their frequency
I trust that you will pardon me;
With French it's spotted like a leopard –
Although I've glanced at, in times gone,
The Academic lexicon.

But never mind, let's rather hurry
Off to the ball as is required,
Whither Onegin in a flurry
Is dashing in the cab he hired.
Along dark streets wrapped deep in slumber
Gay carriages, a goodly number,
Shed rainbow lights across the snow
From their twin lanterns as they go.
With lampions bright on sills and ledges
The splendid mansion shines and gleams,
And silhouetted by the beams,
Across the pane a shadow edges:
The profile that a move will blur
Of lovely lady, modish sir.

Straight past the porter, like an arrow
Our hero took the marble stair,
But then he paused, and with his narrow
White hand he swiftly smoothed his hair,
And entered. Here the throng is trooping;
The orchestra's already drooping;
A gay mazurka holds the crowd;
The press is thick, the hubbub loud.
The Horse Guard's spurs clank as he dances;
And hand meets hand, and hearts beat high;
The ladies' little feet fly by,
Pursued in flight by flaming glances;
While wildly all the fiddles sing
To drown the jealous whispering.

When I knew ardour and elation,
On balls I also used to dote:
There one can make a declaration,
And cleverly convey a note.
Husbands esteemed, to you I tender –
Your honour's most astute defender –
My services in time of need:
My earnest counsels prithee heed
And guard your daughters more severely,
You mothers, as your own once did,
Or else – or else – else God forbid!
Hold your lorgnette up, watch them nearly.
These warnings in your ears are dinned
Because it's long since I have sinned.

Obeying folly's least suggestion,
How much of life I spent in vain,
And yet, were morals not in question,
I'd live through every ball again.
I love fierce youth, my private passion
Is the shrewd elegance of fashion,
The crowd whose sparkle nothing dims,
The little feet and lovely limbs;
Search Russia through, you'll scarce discover
Three pairs of truly pretty feet.
Ah, once how fast my heart would beat
When two feet tripped towards their lover!
I'm sad and cold, and yet it seems
They still can thrill me in my dreams.

When will you lose remembrance of them?
Where go, you madman, to forget?
Ah, little feet, how I did love them!
Now on what flowers are they set?
In Orient luxury once cherished,
The trace you left has long since perished
From northern snows; you loved to tread
Upon voluptuous rugs instead.
It was for you that I neglected
The call of fame, for you forgot
My country, and an exile's lot –
All thoughts but those of you rejected.
Brief as your footprints on the grass,
The happiness of youth must pass.

Diana's breast, the face of Flora,
Are charming, friends, but I would put
Them both aside and only for a
Glimpse of Terpischore's sweet foot.
Prophetic of a priceless pleasure,
A clue to joys beyond all measure,
Its classic grace draws in its wake
Desires that are too keen to slake.
Where'er it goes, I am its lover:
When on the grass in spring it's pressed,
Or by the fireplace set at rest,
At table, 'neath the damask cover,
Crossing the ballroom's polished floor,
Or climbing down the rocky shore.

Well I remember waves in riot
Before a storm; I wanted, too,
Thus to rush forth, then lapse in quiet
There at her feet, as they would do.
I longed to be the waves caressing
Those feet my lips should have been pressing!
No, when with youth and love on fire,
I did not ache with such desire
To brush the shy lips of a maiden
Or touch to flame a rosy cheek,
Or with such urgent ardour seek
To kiss the breast with languor laden;
No, passion never wrought for me
The same consuming agony.

With sighs I think, bemused adorer,
Aghast at time's swift slipping sands,
How once I held her stirrup for her,
And caught that foot in these two hands;
Again, imagination's kindled,
The heart that thought its fires had dwindled
Flames up, the embers glow again
With sudden passion, sudden pain . . .
But in their praises why be stringing
Anew the garrulous fond lyre?
The haughty creatures may inspire
Our songs, but are not worth the singing.
Their looks enchant, their words are sweet,
And quite as faithless as their feet.

And what of my Onegin? Drowsing,
He's driven from the ball to bed:
The drum is heard, the city's rousing,
For Petersburg's no sleepyhead.
The peddler plods, the merchant dresses,
While into town the milkmaid presses,
Bearing her jar o'er creaking snows;
And to his stand the cabby goes.
The cheerful morning sounds awaken;
The shutters open; chimneys spout;
The baker's wicket opens out,
A loaf is proffered, coins are taken,
A white cap shows, all in a trice:
The baker's German and precise.

The ball's wild gaiety was wearing,
So turning morning into night,
To darkness' kind abode repairing,
Now sleeps the scion of delight.
By afternoon he will be waking,
He'll then resume till day is breaking
The merry and monotonous round,
And then once more till noon sleep sound.
But was true joy to Eugene granted
Then, in the flower of his youth?
Was pleasure *happiness* in sooth
'Mid all the conquests that he vaunted?
When in the banquet-hall he beamed
Was he the carefree soul he seemed?

No, soon the world began to bore him,
The senses soon grew blunt and dull,
In vain the belles might clamour for him,
He found the fairest faces null;
Seduction ceased to be amusing,
And friendship's claims he was refusing,
Because he could make no *bon mot*,
Could not wash down with Veuve Clicquot
The beefsteak and the Strasbourg patty
When his poor head began to ache;
And though he was an ardent rake,
An exquisite both bold and natty,
The time came when he quite abhorred
Even the pistol and the sword.

But there's no need that I dissemble
His illness – name it how you choose,
The English *spleen* it may resemble,
'Twas in a word the Russian blues.
He spared us, true, one piece of folly;
Although he grew more melancholy,
Was bored with everything he tried,
He did stop short of suicide.
Soft glance, nor welcome sweetly caroled,
Nor cards, nor gossip, chased his gloom;
He'd stroll into the drawing-room
Surly and languid as Childe Harold.
A wanton sigh was not worth mention:
Nothing attracted his attention.

He first abandoned you, capricious
Great ladies, of whom he'd been fond;
Indeed, today there is a vicious
Ennui pervading the *haut monde*.
Perhaps some lady may find matter
In Say and Bentham for her chatter,
But the discussions I have heard,
Though innocent, are quite absurd.
If you have any mind to flirt, you
Are turned by one cool glance to ice,
So pious are they, so precise,
And so inflexible their virtue.
They are so clever, so serene,
The sight of them produces spleen.

43

You also, youthful belles, belated
O'er Petersburg's dark pavements borne
In dashing cabs, you too were fated
To learn my Eugene's air of scorn.
To stormy gaiety a traitor,
Onegin now decides he'll cater
To an ambitious author's whims:
His door he locks, his lamp he trims.
He yawns, for serious labour tries him,
His page is empty as can be,
The pen makes mock of such as he,
And so the bumptious guild denies him;
And I can't say the clique is wrong
To which, God help me, I belong.

At length our hollow-hearted hero
A worthy course of action finds:
The sum of all his thoughts is zero,
And so he'll rifle keener minds;
A shelf of books he's been perusing,
But who does that is only choosing
Between a rascal and a bore;
He's read and read, and pray, what for?
Old fogies all, chained to tradition,
The newcomers but ape the old;
Behind the curtain's funeral fold
He soon consigns them to perdition.
He's done with women, and it looks
As though he's surely done with books.

The *beau monde*'s burdensome conventions
I too had dropped, and found him then –
As bored as I with vain inventions –
The most congenial of men.
His way of dreaming, willy-nilly,
His sharp intelligence and chilly,
I liked, and his peculiar pose;
I was embittered, he morose.
We both had played with passion, early
We both had wearied of the game;
The hearts of both now spurned the flame
And had grown ashen-cold and surly;
And both, though young, could but await
Men's malice and the stroke of Fate.

One who has lived and thought, grows scornful,
Disdain sits silent in his eye;
One who has felt, is often mournful,
Disturbed by ghosts of days gone by:
He can no longer be enchanted,
No respite to his heart is granted –
Remembering the past, perforce
He is the victim of remorse.
All this lends charm to conversation,
And though the talk of my young friend
At first disturbed me, in the end
I listened, not without elation,
To his sharp judgements, sullen wit,
And epigrams that scored a hit.

Of quiet summer nights, how often,
When with diaphanous pale light
O'er the Neva the sky would soften
And the smooth waters, mirror-bright,
Would fail to show Diana gleaming,
We yielded to delicious dreaming,
Recalling in the soft sweet air
Many a distant love-affair –
The pleasures relished, triumphs thwarted;
Like prisoners released in sleep
To roam the forests, green and deep,
We were in reverie transported,
And carried to that region where
All life before us still lay fair.

Onegin leaned above the river
Upon the granite parapet,
As did the bard – yet not aquiver
With ecstasy, but with regret.
Here one heard naught but echoes, dying,
From distant streets where cabs were flying,
And sentinel to sentinel
Sounding the cry that all was well;
Alone a lazy boatman lifted
His oars above the drowsy stream;
A horn rang out, as in a dream;
A song across the waters drifted;
But Tasso's murmured octaves are,
By night, in dalliance, sweeter far.

· 49

Oh, waters of the Adriatic!
Oh, Brenta! I shall yet rejoice
When once again, inspired, ecstatic,
I hear the magic of your voice,
Sacred to scions of Apollo!
No bard was keen as I to follow
The strains of Albion's proud lyre
Extolling you in tones of fire!
Once free, and night will find me gloating
Upon a fair Venetian face,
Within the gondola's embrace
In golden languor vaguely floating;
And she will learn my knowledge of
The tongue of Petrarch and of love.

'Tis time to loose me from my tether;
I call on freedom – naught avails:
I pace the beach, await good weather,
And beckon to the passing sails.
When, wrapped in storm, shall I be battling
The billows, while the shrouds are rattling,
And roam the sea's expanse, unpent,
Quit of the shore's dull element?
'Tis time to seek the southern surges
Beneath my Afric's sunny sky,
And, there at home, for Russia sigh,
Lamenting in new songs and dirges
The land that knew my love, my pain,
Where long my buried heart has lain.

The pair of us had planned to wander,
On foreign scenes to feast our eyes;
But I am here and he is yonder:
Fate had arranged it otherwise.
Upon the death of his dear father
The creditors began to gather,
And Eugene, when he saw these sirs –
Each man must do as he prefers –
Because he hated litigation
Surrendered his inheritance;
He thought it no great loss – perchance
He had some other expectation?
Had Eugene, from a little bird,
Of his old uncle's illness heard?

Indeed, he soon received a letter
Which told him that his uncle lay
Too ill for hopes of getting better,
And had his last farewells to say.
Eugene perused the sad epistle;
Thoughts of the future made him whistle;
He caught the post with eager haste,
But soon was yawning while he raced:
He knew the task would sorely try him
For (as I've said) there he must sit
And fawn and play the hypocrite.
But when he comes they notify him
His uncle's in his coffin laid:
His debt to nature has been paid.

The servants gave him all assistance,
The house hummed like a hive of bees
With friends and foes come from a distance
Just to enjoy the obsequies.
The dead man buried, they were able
To do full justice to the table,
And, feeling they had done their best,
Gravely departed priest and guest.
Here was Onegin, then, possessing
His stables, forests, streams and land,
He who could never understand
An ordered way of life, confessing
His early years were all a waste,
And this routine was to his taste.

54

Two days he found it quite diverting:
The meadows' solitary look,
The shady thickets' cool, begirting
The babble of a gentle brook;
The third day interest abated
And he was not the least elated
By grove and stream and field and steep –
They only sent him off to sleep.
For though the country boasts no palace,
No card-game, poetry, or ball,
Its pleasures, like the city's, pall,
He noted with accustomed malice.
A shadow, or a wife, pursues
As he was followed by the blues.

55

I like a life of country quiet;
There may the lyre sound clear and free,
There fancies bloom and dreams run riot –
It suits my Muse as it suits me.
At peace, it is my artless pleasure
To wander by the lake at leisure,
In solitude without a flaw,
And *far niente* is my law.
Each morning I awake proposing
Another day without an aim;
I have no care for flighty fame;
I hardly read, I'm often dozing.
Was it not thus I long since spent
My youth in slothful sweet content?

To love and idleness devoted,
To flowery field and village sport,
With pleasure I have often noted
That I am not Onegin's sort;
Let no sly reader be so daring –
Onegin's traits with mine comparing –
And no calumnious friend so pert
As some time later to assert
That here, for all the world to know it,
I've drawn a likeness perfectly:
A portrait of none else but me,
Like Byron, pride's consummate poet;
As though there were a tacit ban
On writing of another man.

Poets, it is my observation,
Indulge in lovers' dreams with ease;
I too made it my occupation
To play with tender reveries.
First memory would trace the features,
In secret, of dear distant creatures,
And the rare magic of the Muse
The breath of life would then infuse.
The mountain maid, untamed, inspiring,
The prisoned girls of the Salgir,
'Twas thus I sang them – both were dear.
Now my companions are inquiring:
'In all the jealous crowd, what she
Commands your tender minstrelsy?

' Whose glances, quickening emotion,
Caressingly repaid your song?
To whom did your confessed devotion,
To whom your pensive verse belong?'
To no one, friends, you must believe me:
I loved, and nothing could relieve me.
That man alone knows blessedness
Who is inspired in his distress:
For thus he brings his passion's fuel
To poetry's exalted flame;
And when consoled by art – and fame,
Like Petrarch, he finds love less cruel.
But, feeling the blind archer's sting,
I was a dolt and could not sing.

The Muse has come, and love departed,
The darkened mind is clear again;
And as of old I mix, free-hearted,
Feeling and thought with music's strain.
I write, and longing is diminished;
Beside the stanza all unfinished
No more the casual pen is led
To sketch a woman's legs or head.
Cold ashes hide no smouldering ember;
I have no tears, in spite of grief;
The storms which shook it like a leaf
Soon, soon my soul will not remember:
Then what a poem I'll contrive
In cantos numbering twenty-five!

The plan I had no pains to settle,
The hero's named, the work's begun;
My novel finds me in good fettle
And I've completed Chapter One.
I've scanned the pages most severely,
The errors are a trifle merely,
And those I do not greatly rue;
I'll give the censorship its due,
Let critics wreak their indignation
Upon the finished product then;
Neva, oh, offspring of my pen,
Shall greet you. Go, my dear creation:
Be sentenced by a crooked jury
And earn me fame and sound and fury.

CHAPTER TWO

O rus!
HORACE

O Rus!

I

The village where Onegin's leisure
But left him bored to a degree
Would ravish one who prized the treasure
Of innocent felicity.
The mansion, by a hill well hidden,
Where winds and tempests were forbidden,
And near a stream, stood calm and proud,
Surveying fallow land and ploughed.
Beyond, the plain, with hamlets dotted,
And chequered brown and gold and green,
A halcyon bucolic scene,
With roaming flocks was lightly spotted;
While in the garden's lavish shade
The contemplative dryads played.

The mansion from its firm foundation
Up to its roof was past all praise,
Expressing the discrimination,
The noble taste of bygone days.
The stove with coloured tiles, appealing
If out of date, the lofty ceiling,
Ancestral portraits in the gloom
And damask of the drawing-room –
All this is now outworn and faded,
The glory's gone, I know not why;
But the sad ruin brought no sigh
From Eugene: he was far.too jaded –
In time-worn halls and those that just
Had been refurbished, yawn he must.

3

The room where the old man berated
His housekeeper for forty years,
Killed flies, and snugly rusticated
Is now our hero's, it appears.
The furnishings are plain and stable:
Two chests, a down-stuffed couch, a table;
The floor is oak; and do not think
That you will find one spot of ink.
Onegin searched the cupboards, finding
Liqueurs, a ledger, applejack,
And, tucked away, an almanac
For 1808 without a binding:
The old man had no time to look
Into a more exacting book.

Alone among his new possessions,
At first Eugene began to dream
Of making certain grand concessions
And setting up a new régime;
For the corvée he substituted
Light quit-rent, and the slave, well suited
Because there was not much to pay,
Blessed the new master every day.
Not so his calculating neighbour
Who thought our Eugene was a gull;
Another neighbour tapped his skull:
Why thus dispense with lawful labour?
The youth was called on every hand
A faddist and a firebrand.

The neighbours promptly called and twaddled
Of this and that, to his distress;
Hence oft he had his stallion saddled
At the back porch in readiness,
That he, when wheels were within hearing,
Might dash away as they were nearing.
The gentry all cried out in scorn,
This insult was not to be borne.
'Onegin is a boor, a mason;
He leaves the ladies' hands unkissed;
Drinks wine in tumblers,' it was hissed;
'He never puts a civil face on,
Says, "yes" and "no", but never "sir".'
In this opinion all concur.

Another landowner come newly
To his estate, which was quite near,
Was also picked to pieces duly,
For his good neighbours found him queer:
Vladimir Lensky, handsome, youthful,
A Kantian, unspoiled and truthful,
Whose soul was shaped in Göttingen,
And who could wield a poet's pen.
From misty Germany Vladimir
Had brought the fruit of learning's tree:
An ardent faith in liberty,
The spirit of an oddish dreamer,
An eloquent and eager tongue,
Black curls that to his shoulder hung.

Unspoiled by the vain show and fleeting
Of this cold world, his soul would bless
With equal warmth a comrade's greeting
And a shy maiden's pure caress.
His heart the nest of fond illusion,
In worldly dazzle and confusion
The hopeful youth was quick to find
Much to enchant his virgin mind.
His doubts were never past the curing,
In reverie they would dissolve;
Life was a riddle he would solve,
He found it puzzling but alluring;
He racked his brains, and still believed
That miracles could be achieved.

8

A kindred soul, he held, was burning
To be united to his own,
And day by day in pensive yearning
It waited on, for him alone;
He held that loyal friends and steady
To save his honour stood quite ready
To suffer prison, and would fly
At once the slanderer to defy.
He held that some by Fate were chosen

....
....
....
....
....

9

He early knew the agitation
Of love for virtue, sore regret,
The stir of noble indignation,
Hope of a name none might forget.
He was none of your poetasters,
Goethe and Schiller were his masters,
Beneath their sky he plucked his lyre,
His spirit knew their lyric fire.
And, fortune's darling, in his rhyming
He paid the Muses honour due;
His sentiments were fine and true,
His music therewith sweetly chiming;
His were the dreams that move the heart
And his the charm of simple art.

The theme from which he ne'er departed
Was love: he sang it late and soon,
Serene as maidens simple-hearted,
As infant slumbers, as the moon
In the unruffled heavens shining;
He sang of parting and repining;
The mystic, wistful hours of night;
Of distance, promising delight;
He sang the rose, romantic flower;
And lands remote, where on the breast
Of silence he had lain at rest
And let his tears unheeded shower;
He sang life's bloom and early blight:
His nineteenth year was scarce in sight.

11

Eugene alone was framed to measure
The gifts the newcomer possessed;
The local gentry's round of pleasure
Could scarce inspire young Lensky's zest.
He fled their noisy conversation
And found their prudent talk vexation:
All kin and kennels, crops and wine;
Here not a wit was found to shine
(Not with fine words are parsnips buttered);
No syllable of sentiment,
No grace, no flash of merriment,
Lay hid in all the prose they uttered, –
No *savoir vivre*, no hint of verse;
And when their wives talked, it was worse.

Lensky was thought an eligible,
A wealthy youth and handsome too;
There *was* something intelligible
About this common rustic view;
The talk would turn with strange persistence
Upon the bachelor's sad existence;
All wish to see their daughters wed
To this half-Russian, German-bred.
The samovar, that blest invention,
Is brought, and Dunya pours his tea;
And next the girl's guitar we see;
They whisper: 'Dunya, pay attention!'
And Dunya squeaks (would she were dumb!)
'*Into my golden chamber, come!*'

Of course young Lensky felt no yearning
For marriage bond or marriage bell;
Instead of that, our friend was burning
To know Onegin really well.
They met; except that both were human,
They were unlike as any two men:
As rock and wave, or ice and flame,
Or prose and verse – in naught the same.
So different, first they bored each other,
Then liking grew: they met each day
On horseback; such close friends were they,
They clung as brother clings to brother.
Thus people, frankly I confess,
Grow fond – out of sheer idleness.

Such faithful friendship as my hero's
Is in these parlous days unknown;
We think all other people zeros,
And integers: ourselves alone.
We're all Napoleons, we're certain –
On sentiment we draw the curtain;
Two-legged millions are our tools;
Emotion is for clowns and fools.
Eugene, more tolerant than many,
Yet, as a rule, despised mankind;
Exceptions may be hard to find
But there's no rule that has not any:
He scorned most men (not everyone),
Esteemed emotion, feeling none.

He listened to young Lensky, smiling:
The poet's ardent speech, the mind
So immature and so beguiling,
The fiery glance, he could but find
A novelty framed to divert him;
He thought: I must not disconcert him
By mocking glance or chilly word,
Such bliss is transient, if absurd;
Since time, without my interference,
Will cure the lad, for good or ill,
Let him believe in wonders still
And credit the world's fair appearance;
Youth's fever is its own excuse
For ravings that it may induce.

In deep reflection, hot discussion,
Their meetings passed; in turn they spoke
Of foreign history and Russian,
Of prejudice's ancient yoke,
Of good and evil, and of science,
Of destiny and its defiance,
Of that dread mystery, the grave;
Their judgement both men freely gave.
The poet in his exaltation
Would cite a verse he had by heart,
Some fragment of his northern art,
And clinch the point with a quotation.
Though Eugene lent a willing ear,
He found the matter not too clear.

The passions, though, concerned more often
Our talkative young eremites;
Onegin's mocking voice would soften
As he depicted their delights;
He sighed, no longer subject to them:
Most blessed is he who never knew them,
And blessed the man who rids him of
Their pangs! and he, remote from love,
Who never longed and never hated,
Who, yawning, with his friends and wife,
In gossip finds the spice of life,
All jealous thoughts evaporated –
The happy man who took no chance
At cards with his inheritance!

When we seek refuge, growing colder,
Beneath the prudent flag of peace,
When passion's fires no longer smoulder,
And all their wayward stirrings cease,
And when we find our old devotion
No more a reason for emotion,
And its late sequel as absurd,
We yet attend upon the word
That trembles with another's passion;
The heart recalls its ancient scars,
As one who fought forgotten wars
Reviews the past in wistful fashion:
A veteran who never fails
To hang upon the young bloods' tales.

But fiery youth cannot dissemble
Its love or anger, grief or joy;
It all pours forth from lips that tremble
With the avowals of a boy.
Wearing a look of self-possession,
Onegin heard the sweet confession
His friend unburdened himself of –
He was a veteran in love.
Freely the poet spoke and truly,
His heart was pure, his conscience clear;
Onegin was allowed to hear
In full the tender story duly,
A tale of sentiment not new,
These many years, to me, or you.

He loved as people love no longer
Whose hearts the years at length anneal;
His was the love of poets, stronger
Than other men are doomed to feel:
He knew one constant inspiration,
And not long years of separation,
Nor distance, changed his earnest mood
Or brought his longing quietude.
Not hours when he fulfilled the duties
That poets owe unto the Muse,
Nor studies such as pedants choose,
Nor noisy games, nor foreign beauties,
Could alter Lensky's virgin soul
Where love burned like a living coal.

When scarce a lad, his heart was captured –
A heart that had not felt a pang –
By little Olga, and, enraptured,
He watched her as she played and sang;
And one would find the children roaming
Together in the forest gloaming;
The fathers, indeed all, could see
Their marriage was a certainty.
Watched fondly, in seclusion growing,
The charming and ingenuous maid
Bloomed like a flower in the shade;
A lily of the valley blowing
In the thick grass where none can see,
Unknown to butterfly and bee.

The poet's earliest elation
Young Olga was the first to stir;
She was his lyre's first inspiration,
His virgin lyric was of her.
But now adieu, oh, golden playtime!
He loved the dark and shunned the daytime,
And craved the forest's shady boon,
The silent stars, the brooding moon –
The moon, the lampion of heaven,
To which we vowed our walks apart,
Whose secret solace on the heart
Would drop so tenderly at even . . .
Though now a light of no repute,
The street-lamps' pallid substitute.

Sweet as the kiss of love and simple
As Lensky's life that knew no guile
Was gentle Olga – in her dimple
One saw the cheerful morning smile;
Her sky-blue eyes, her cheeks like roses,
Her flaxen hair, her graceful poses,
Her voice, were such as they portray
In all the novels of the day.
There was a time when such a picture
Was one that I found exquisite,
But now I am fed up with it;
Dear reader, pray forgive the stricture,
And I shall speak, if you allow,
About her elder sister now.

Though it suggests a peasant's hovel,
Tatyana was her sister's name:
For the first time in any novel
It humbly asks romantic fame.
Why not? You can have no objection,
Though it is true your recollection
Of syllables so musical
Is bound up with the servants' hall,
With olden days and doddering nurses;
We can't please the fastidious,
For there's a lack of taste in us,
And in our names (and in our verses);
Enlightenment makes such as we
No finer, but just finicky.

Tatyana was her name then – granted.
She would not win you by her face,
She lacked her sister's charm, and wanted
Her rosy innocence and grace.
No, silent, wild, and melancholy,
And swift to flee from fun and folly,
Shy as the doe who runs alone,
She seemed a stranger to her own.
To fondle either parent never
Was our morose Tatyana's way,
And as a child she'd romp and play
With other children scarcely ever,
But by the window she would brood
The whole day through in solitude.

Since infancy her only pleasure
Was reverie; she wreathed with dream
The placid course of rustic leisure;
Her tender fingers sewed no seam,
Nor was she found with head inclining
O'er her embroidery, designing
In coloured silks a pattern fit
To make a guest exclaim at it.
The will to rule is seen thus early:
The child while still at play prepares
For all her future social cares
And the polite world's hurly-burly.
And tells her doll with anxious thought
The maxims her mamma has taught.

But even then, and more's the pity,
Tatyana had no doll at all
To gossip to about the city
And what the fashions were that fall.
She was not one of those who glories
In mischief, but horrific stories
Enchanted her while yet a child,
In winter when the nights were wild.
And when the little girls collected
To tag each other, or to roam
The woods, Tatyana stayed at home,
By solitude nowise dejected;
Her dreamy mood did not consort
With laughter and with noisy sport.

Tatyana dearly loved romancing
Upon her balcony alone
Just as the stars had left off dancing,
When dawn's first ray had barely shown;
When the cool messenger of morning,
The wind, would enter, gently warning
That day advancing, brisk and bright,
Would soon supplant this pallid light.
In winter, when night's shade encloses
More lingeringly half the world,
And in the misty moonlight furled,
The lazy Orient longer dozes,
Roused at her wonted hour from rest,
By candle-light she rose and dressed.

She found in a romantic story
All one might care to be or know;
She lived the chapters, and would glory
In Richardson and in Rousseau.
Her father saw no harm in reading
(He was a decent chap, conceding
He lived in quite another age);
But then he never read a page.
He did not know that books could say things
To move you even while you slept;
He thought the tomes his daughter kept
Beneath her pillow, empty playthings;
While, on the other hand, his wife
Held Richardson as dear as life.

The lady's lasting admiration
The novelist had long since won;
She had not read with fascination
Of Lovelace or of Grandison,
But she had heard of them a dozen
Or more times from her Moscow cousin,
Princess Aline, when she was young,
And when, besides, her heart was wrung:
She was affianced, but her mother
Had made the choice, 'twas not her own;
Her heart was filled with one alone,
For, sad to say, she loved another:
A Grandison attached to cards,
A beau, a sergeant of the Guards.

She followed, as he did, the fashion;
On elegance her mind was bent.
But what availed her urgent passion?
They married her *sans* her consent.
Her prudent husband, to distract her,
Off to the country promptly packed her,
Hoping her grief might thus abate;
They settled down on his estate,
Where she, with God knows who for neighbours,
At first but wept and tore her hair,
Spoke of divorce in her despair,
Then plunged into domestic labours
Content, since habit, more or less,
Is surrogate for happiness.

Kind habit soothed her sorrow sweetly,
Until a great discovery
Consoled the lady and completely
Restored her equanimity.
Between her hours of toil and leisure
The good wife took her husband's measure,
And learned to rule the roost herself.
She kept control of house and pelf;
She shipped as a recruit the peasant
She best could spare; she kept the books,
And pickled mushrooms with her cooks;
Slapped servant girls who were unpleasant;
And steamed herself on Saturday –
Her spouse had not a word to say.

Time was when lines that she indited
In albums, writ in blood, were seen;
She spoke in sing-song and delighted
To call Praskovya 'Pauline';
She pinched her waist with tightened laces,
Affected a most nasal 'n';
But years were rolling by, and then
She lost her Frenchy airs and graces;
The album and the corset vanished,
The tender verse, Princesse Pauline;
She said 'Akulka' for Céline;
The nasal twang she also banished,
And wore, her last defences down,
A mob-cap and a wadded gown.

But her good husband loved her dearly,
And let her put him on the shelf;
He never looked at her too nearly
And lolled in dishabille himself;
His life, that knew no cares or labours,
Rolled by in peace; at times, the neighbours,
Some friendly family, at eve,
Dropped in to gossip, laugh or grieve
Together o'er some simple matter;
And time would pass, and there would be
Young Olga coming to make tea,
And put a finis to their chatter;
They'd sup, then time for sleep drew nigh,
And so the guests would say good-bye.

They kept the good old ways and wallowed
At Carnival in savoury cheer,
Eating the pancakes custom hallowed;
They took communion twice a year;
At Christmas carols were their pleasure;
They liked to tread a country measure;
At Whitsun, when the populace
Yawned through the long thanksgiving Mass,
To sentiment the pair conceded
A tear upon the kingcups shed;
To certain habits they were wed;
As men need air, 'twas *kvass* they needed;
Liked hearty guests who ate and drank,
And served each course to them by rank.

And so they aged, like all things mortal,
And in due time the husband passed
Submissive through the grave's dark portal,
And wore the funeral wreath at last.
A tender father, a good master,
His passing came as a disaster
To friend and child and faithful wife;
He'd led a kind and simple life;
He died a short hour before dinner.
His epitaph is plain as he;
Graved on the monument you see:
'Dmitry Larin, a poor sinner,
God's servant, and a brigadier,
Come to eternal rest, lies here.'

At home again, young Lensky duly
Beheld the bed where all must lie,
And by those ashes, mourning truly,
Paid them the tribute of a sigh.
'Alas, poor Yorick!' he lamented,
'Once in those arms I lay contented,
And took his medal for a toy
When I was but a tiny boy!
He hoped that in good time I'd marry
His Olga. I can hear him say:
"May I but live to see the day!
When we were young, we did not tarry."'
And Lensky, grieving honestly,
Wrote, on the spot, an elegy.

38

And there he also wrote another
Upon the patriarchal dust,
And wept his father and his mother . . .
Alas! by God's strange will we must
Behold each generation flourish,
And watch life's furrows briefly nourish
The perishable human crop,
Which ripens fairly, but to drop;
And where one falls, another surges . . .
The race of men recks nothing, save
Its reckless growth: into the grave
The grandfathers it promptly urges.
Our time will come when it is due,
Our grandchildren evict us too.

39

Meanwhile, forget all toil and trouble,
Take what is offered of delight.
I know that life is but a bubble,
My fondness for it is but slight;
I am deceived by no illusion;
But I salute hope's shy intrusion,
And sometimes in my heart I own
I would not leave the world, unknown.
I have no faith in its requiting
My labours, yet perhaps this name
May wear the laurel-crown of fame,
And yet win lustre from my writing;
One line, held in the memory,
May speak, like a fond friend, of me.

My words may move some unborn lover;
My stanza, saved by jealous fate,
It may be Lethe will not cover;
Ah, yes, at some far distant date,
When I am gone, and cannot know it,
The cordial words: 'There was a poet!'
Some dunce may yet pronounce as he
Points out my portrait unctuously.
Such are the bard's gratifications;
My thanks, friend, you will not refuse,
You venerator of the Muse
Who will recall my poor creations,
You who will smooth in after days
With kindly hand the old man's bays.

CHAPTER THREE

Elle étoit fille, elle étoit amoureuse
MALFILÂTRE

I

'These poets! What! another visit?'
'Good-bye, Onegin, I must go.'
'I shan't detain you; but where is it
  You spend your time, I'd like to know?'
'These evenings? At the Larins'.' 'Splendid.
  But, Lord, before the evening's ended
  How is it that you do not fall
  Asleep from boredom?' 'Not at all.'
'I cannot grasp it. I'll be betting
  Here's what you find there (am I right?):
  The guests are greeted with delight;
  You have a Russian family setting,
  With tea and jam, and endless tattle
  About the weather, flax, and cattle . . .'

[68]

'I see no harm in that; I'm grateful.'
'But it's a bore, my friend, that's clear.'
'Your fashionable world is hateful;
I find the plain home circle dear,
Where I can . . .' 'Ah, another pretty
Bucolic piece! Good Lord, have pity!
Well, must you go now? Not so fast!
When shall I meet the girl at last
Whom you have found so interesting?
I'd like to see with my own eyes
Your Phyllis, whom you idolize.
Pray introduce me.' 'You are jesting.'
'No.' 'Gladly.' 'When?' 'At once. You'll see
How very welcome you will be.'

3

'Let's go.'
        The friends, without delaying,
Dashed off; arrived; and heartily
Were greeted, with almost dismaying
Old-fashioned hospitality.
The table shone with wax; they handed
The saucers of preserve about,
Set lingonberry syrup out,
Just as the social rites demanded.

. . . .
. . . .
. . . .
. . . .
. . . .
. . . .

4

They travel homeward quickly, choosing,
For it is late, the shortest way;
And reader, you are not refusing
To overhear what they may say.
'Well, now, Onegin. Yawning?' 'Merely
A habit, Lensky.' 'Oh, but clearly,
You're bored.' 'As ever. But I mark
That we are driving in the dark.
Be quick! Drive on!' he bids the peasant;
'This silly landscape! Never mind;
Your Madam Larina's, I find,
A nice old woman, plain but pleasant.
That lingonberry syrup will,
I've a suspicion, make me ill.

5

'But tell me, which one is Tatyana?'
'She sat beside the window. She
Is like the poet's maid, Svetlana,
Given to mournful reverie.'
'You love the younger? Curious creature!'
'Why do you say so?' 'Not a feature
Of Olga's looks alive to me.
Her sister tempts the Muse, not she.
Your Olga's face, so round and blooming,
Is like Van Dyck's Madonna. Fie!
Or like, up in the silly sky,
That silly moon you see there looming.'
Vladimir made a dry response.

The neighbours, pleasantly diverted,
Asked what Onegin's visit meant,
And one and all of them exerted
Themselves to find out his intent.
Tatyana's match was all the rumour;
They gossiped on, in high good humour,
If there was carping comment, too;
And there were those who said they knew
The plans to have been consummated.
But that the wedding was deferred
Because they lacked – hadn't you heard? –
The rings that the new mode dictated.
Of Lensky's troth there was no chatter:
His wedding was a settled matter.

Tatyana listened with vexation
To gossip; but her heart would fill
With a strange, secret exultation;
She conned the talk against her will;
A thought was born, and grew, unbidden;
Thus grows a seed the earth has hidden
When springtime's sun shines warm above:
The time had come – she was in love.
Long since her dreams had set her yearning
And coveting the fatal food;
Long since with sweet disquietude
Had her shy wistful heart been burning;
And freighted with a youthful gloom
Her soul was waiting . . . ah, for whom?

He came. And her eyes opened. Quaking,
She whispered to herself: 'Tis he!
Alas, in dreams, asleep or waking,
From thoughts of him she is not free;
All speaks of him, but to confound her;
His magic presence hovers round her;
And so from idle talk she flies,
And from the servants' anxious eyes.
Plunged into sadness beyond measure,
When guests arrive she pays no heed,
But wishes them away with speed,
And curses their unwelcome leisure;
She hates their having come at all,
Their endlessly protracted call.

With what devoted concentration
She reads the sweet romance, and how
Discovers a new fascination
In its seductive figments now!
The creatures fancy animated:
Werther, to be a martyr fated,
Malek-Adhel and de Linar,
The lover of Julie Wolmar,
And Grandison, who leaves us sleeping,
The matchless bore – on these she mused;
And all, our tender dreamer fused
Into one image, her heart leaping
As fancy in the lot would trace
Onegin's form, Onegin's face.

And so her quick imagination
Reveals herself in every scene;
She is the novelist's creation:
Julie, Clarissa, or Delphine;
She wanders with imagined lovers
Through silent woods, and she discovers
Her dreams in every circumstance
Of some imported wild romance.
Another's joy her heart possesses,
Another's grief is hers to rue,
And in her mind a *billet doux*
To her dear hero she addresses.
The hero we're intent upon,
However, was no Grandison.

There was a time when the impassioned
Romancer, having settled on
A noble style of writing, fashioned
The pattern of a paragon.
His soul by highest motives guided,
The darling object was provided
With a fine mind and handsome face;
His enemies were always base.
This ever-rapturous hero, burning
With pure devotion, knew no bliss
As exquisite as sacrifice;
And to the final pages turning,
You'd find the way of vice was hard,
And virtue won its due reward.

But now all minds are fogged and cloudy,
We're put to sleep by moral tales;
We like romances not too rowdy
Wherein agreeable vice prevails.
The British Muse's wild invention
Lays claim to the young girl's attention;
Dark Melmoth fills her with delight;
The Vampire wrecks her sleep at night;
She loves the secrets that environ
The Corsair or the Wandering Jew;
Strange Jean Sbogar enchants her too.
By a most happy whim, Lord Byron
Has clothed a hopeless egoism
In saturnine romanticism.

All this is futile, and you know it,
My friends. Perhaps, by heaven's decree,
I shall yet cease to be a poet;
Another demon seizing me,
I shall defy the dread Apollo,
Content in my old age to follow
The fashion of an older day:
Write prose, and take the humbler way;
I'll tell no ghostly tales, or gory,
Or paint the villain's agony;
A simple Russian family
Will be the subject of my story,
And love's delicious dream, and, too,
The customs that our fathers knew.

The father's simple words repeating,
Or the old uncle's, I shall tell
Next of the children's breathless meeting,
Where lindens hide the lovers well;
Of jealous pangs, and separation,
And tears of reconciliation
After they've quarrelled once again;
I'll bring them to the altar then . . .
I shall recall the tongue of longing,
The languors of a distant day,
When at my mistress' feet I lay
And to my lips the words came thronging;
The lover's language, the sweet vow,
Of which I've lost the habit now.

Tatyana, dear Tatyana! Weeping,
I share the scalding tears you drop:
Your fate is put into the keeping
Of a most tyrannous young fop.
And you, my dear, are doomed to perish;
But first, what dark delight you cherish,
What dazzling hopes awhile are yours,
As you discover life's allures,
And drink desire's sweet poisoned potion.
You dwell in dreams, and you persist
In fancying a happy tryst
In every nook, with strange emotion;
And everywhere that you may turn
Your marked seducer you discern.

Her grief into the garden taking,
Tatyana goes, impelled by love.
She drops her eyes, her heart is aching,
Her languor will not let her move.
Her eyes shine, and her breath has dwindled,
Her chest heaves, and her cheeks are kindled
With flame that fails as it appears;
There is a roaring in her ears . . .
Night falls; the moon, already riding
Aloft, the whole of heaven sees;
The nightingale's keen melodies
Pour from the boughs where she is hiding.
Sleepless, Tatyana would converse
In gentle whispers with her nurse.

'I cannot sleep, nurse; it is stifling!
  Open the window; come, sit here.'
'What ails you, Tanya?' 'Oh, it's trifling,
  I'm bored; tell me a story, dear.'
'A story?' asked the good old woman,
'Of maids and creatures superhuman?
  Ah, yes, I knew such old wives' tales,
  But I grow old, and memory fails;
  How sad it is to be forgetting!
  I've fallen on black days, my dear –
  I lose the thread, my mind's not clear,
  It is no wonder I am fretting . . . '
'But, nurse, you still can tell me of
  Your own young days. Were you in love?'

'What notions! You may find it blameless,
  But in my youth no one engaged
  In talk of love. It was thought shameless –
  My mother-in-law would have raged.'
'But you were married, nurse,' said Tanya,
'How was it?' 'By God's will, my Vanya
  Was but a boy, if truth were told,
  And I was just thirteen years old.
  The marriage-broker kept on pressing
  The matter for a fortnight; oh,
  What tears I shed you do not know,
  The day my father gave his blessing;
  They loosed my braids, and singing low,
  Led me to church. I had to go.

'I lived, by strangers quite surrounded,
  My husband's folk . . . But do you hear?'
'Ah, nurse, nurse darling, I am hounded
  By longing. I am ill, I fear:
  I want to cry, to sob – oh, nursey!'
'My child, you're ill! The Lord have mercy!
  God grant it's nothing! Welladay!
  How can I help you, only say!
  I'll sprinkle you with holy water,
  You have a fever . . .' 'Fever, no:
  I . . . I'm in love,' she murmured low.
  The nurse replied: 'God save you, daughter!'
  And crossed the girl, and as she made
  The sign with shaking hand, she prayed.

'I am in love,' poor Tanya uttered
 The words again with stifled moan.
'Dear, you are ill,' the old nurse muttered.
'I am in love; leave me alone.'
 Meanwhile, the moon her silver duty
 Performing, lit the girl's pale beauty,
 And with a sombre splendour shone
 On her loose hair, her tears, and on
 The bench where the old nurse was seated
 In kerchief and long gown of wool,
 Before her charge, whose eyes were full,
 Whose posture was of one defeated.
 And while the world in silence slept,
 The moon her magic vigil kept.

 The moon's enchantment so obsessed her,
 Her soul to distant regions fled,
 And then a sudden thought possessed her . . .
'Go, leave me, nurse,' Tatyana said,
'Move up the table, give me paper,
 And pen; good night.' Her single taper
 Is the benign and silent moon;
 Alone, Tatyana broods, and soon
 Propped on her elbow, she is writing,
 Thinking of Eugene all the while.
 A young girl's ardour, clear of guile,
 Breathes through the words she is inditing.
 The letter's ready to be sent;
 For whom, Tatyana, is it meant?

I have known women, stern and rigid,
Great ladies, far too proud to fall,
As pure as winter, and as frigid;
I understood them not at all.
I marvelled at their iron virtue,
Their freezing glances framed to hurt you,
And sooth, I fled these haughty belles
Upon whose brows methought was hell's
Inscription graven plain: 'Surrender
All hope, O ye who enter here.'
They like to fill a man with fear,
And shun the heart that would be tender.
By the Neva it may be you
Have seen such ladies, not a few.

And where the faithful suitor hovers,
I have seen other belles who bent
A glance upon their urgent lovers,
Self-centred and indifferent.
And what was my amazement, finding
They sought to make love's ties more binding
By an assumed austerity;
They schemed to win fidelity:
At least, if pity seemed to soften
Their voices, and their words were kind,
Young love, because it is so blind,
Would grow more ardent very often,
And the fond fool would then pursue
The unconcerned beloved anew.

Why is Tatyana an offender?
Is it because she cannot deem
Deceit exists, but clings with tender
Simplicity to her young dream?
Is it because her love is artless,
And she, not knowing men are heartless,
Obeys her feelings *sans* demur?
Or because Heaven gifted her
With fiery imagination,
With rebel will and lively mind,
And with a heart for love designed,
A spirit brooking no dictation?
And can you not forgive, if she
Shows passion's blind temerity?

Not like a cool coquette who tenders
Her heart, and when she likes, withdraws,
Tatyana like a child surrenders
Herself to love and all its laws.
She does not argue: by delaying
We win the game that we are playing,
And raise love's value cleverly;
First let us prick his vanity
With hope, then prove it an illusion,
Raise doubts that leave his heart perplexed,
With jealousy revive it next,
And thus reduce him to confusion;
Lest, sick of pleasure, momently
The sly thrall struggle to be free.

But I foresee a fresh objection,
And I confess I am perplexed:
Could Russia pardon my defection
Should I not give the letter's text
In Russian? And the task's infernal.
Tatyana read no Russian journal,
She did not speak the language well
And found it rather hard to spell;
And so of course the girl decided
To write in French . . . What's to be done?
For lady never, no, not one,
Her love in Russian has confided;
Our native tongue turns up its nose
At mere epistolary prose.

They say the ladies should read Russian,
But though the arguments are keen,
I cannot suffer the discussion –
To find a Moscow magazine
In those white hands would be distressing!
The fair ones, whom you were addressing
With flattering pen and heart aglow,
Were all of them, as well you know,
My poet friends, inclined to stammer
When they employed the mother-tongue;
We loved them, though, when we were young
For just those little slips of grammar;
The foreign tongue is native to
Those lovely lips; is it not true?

To see a pedant in a bonnet!
A scholar in a yellow shawl!
Pray God I do not come upon it
Where guests disperse, or at a ball!
I hate red lips that are unsmiling,
And likewise do not find beguiling
The sound of Russian when correct;
Slight errors have a choice effect.
Perhaps, heeding the journals' clamour,
The younger beauties will declare
That poetry is their affair,
And will accustom us to grammar;
But as for me . . . my loving praise
Is for the good old-fashioned ways.

My heart will as of old be shaken,
Touched by the careless twittering,
The phrasing, awkward or mistaken,
Of some attractive little thing.
I am not given to repentance –
French turns will please me in a sentence
As do the sins of years long fled
Or light verse that our fathers read.
Enough. 'Tis time that I presented
The letter to you quite intact.
By God! I wish I could retract.
Was ever harder task invented?
Parny's sad tenderness is now
No more the vogue, you will allow.

Singer of feasts and tender sorrow,
If only you were with me still,
I might indeed make bold to borrow
Your magic music and your skill:
Your version of Tatyana's letter
Would be in every way far better
Than anything that I could do –
I bow and cede my rights to you . . .
But no, our paths have separated.
To praises unaccustomed grown,
Beneath the Finnish sky, alone,
Among sad cliffs he moves. I'm fated
To mourn his absence, and in vain,
He does not even guess my pain.

Tatyana's letter lies before me,
I treasure it most piously;
These artless lines can never bore me,
They touch the springs of reverie.
Who taught her how to be so lavish
With ardent words, and how to ravish
The heart with virgin tenderness?
Where did she learn this wild excess?
Love's discourse, perilous, delicious,
She knew, I wonder how. I fear
The version of it given here
Is like a copy pale and vicious,
Or like an air from *Freischütz* played
By someone awkward and afraid.

I write you; is my act not serving
As an avowal? Well I know
The punishment I am deserving:
That you despise me. Even so,
Perhaps for my sad fate preserving
A drop of pity, you'll forbear
To leave me here in my despair.
I first resolved upon refraining
From speech: you never would have learned
The secret shame with which I burned,
If there had been a hope remaining
That I should see you once a week
Or less, that I should hear you speak,
And answer with the barest greeting,
But have one thing when you were gone,
One thing alone to think upon
For days, until another meeting.
But you're unsociable, they say,
The country, and its dullness, bore you;
We . . . We don't shine in any way,
But have a hearty welcome for you.
Why did you come to visit us?
Here in this village unfrequented,
Not knowing you, I would not thus
Have learned how hearts can be tormented,
I might (who knows?) have grown contented,
My girlish dreams forever stilled,
And found a partner in another,
And been a faithful wife and mother,
And loved the duties well fulfilled.

Another? . . . No, my heart is given

To one forever, one alone!
It was decreed . . . The will of Heaven
Ordained it so: I am your own.
All my past life has had one meaning –
That I should meet you. God on high
Has sent you, and I shall be leaning
On your protection till I die . . .
I saw you in my dreams; I'd waken
To know I loved you; long ago
I languished in your glance, and oh!
My soul, hearing your voice, was shaken.
The moment that I saw you coming,
I thrilled, my pulses started drumming,
And my heart whispered: it is he!
Yes, deep within I had the feeling,
When at my tasks of charity,
Or when, the world about me reeling,
I looked for peace in prayer, kneeling,
That silently you spoke to me.
Just now, did I not see you flitting
Through the dim room where I am sitting,
To stand, dear vision, by my bed?
Was it not you who gently gave me
A word to solace and to save me:
The hope on which my heart is fed?
Are you a guardian angel to me
Or but a tempter to undo me?
Dispel my doubts! My mind's awhirl;
Perhaps mere folly has created
These fancies of a simple girl
And quite another end is fated . . .
So be it! Now my destiny
Lies in your hands, for you to fashion;

Forgive the tears you wring from me,
I throw myself on your compassion . . .
Imagine: here I am alone,
With none to understand or cherish
My restless thoughts, and I must perish,
Stifled, in solitude, unknown.
I wait: when once your look has spoken,
My heart once more with hope will glow,
Or a deserved reproach will show
The painful dream forever broken!

Reread I cannot . . . I must end . . .
The fear, the shame, are past endurance . . .
Upon your honour I depend,
And lean upon it with assurance . . .

Tatyana moans, and as she shivers
The letter shakes; she heaves a sigh;
Upon her tongue the wafer quivers –
Both tongue and seal are pink, are dry.
Her nightgown slips from off her shoulder,
And her head sinks. The dawn grows bolder,
And soon the east will be alight;
The moon is fading with the night;
The lifting mist reveals the pleasant
Pale valley and the silver stream;
The first shy rays begin to gleam;
The shepherd's horn awakes the peasant;
'Tis morning; all the world's astir:
It makes no difference to her.

Dawn's air is sweet, she does not feel it,
She sits with downcast head, too lax
To take the letter up and seal it
With her neat monogram in wax.
The old grey nurse thinks she is napping
And enters softly without rapping,
Upon her tray a steaming cup:
'Come now, my child, it's time: get up.
But you're already up! God save me,
You are an early bird! Last night
I left you in a dreadful fright;
But never mind the turn you gave me;
I see the pain has left no trace;
A poppy could not match your face.'

'Ah, nurse, I know you won't refuse me.'
'Of course not, darling, only say . . .'
'Don't think . . . but really . . . don't accuse me . . .
Do me this favour, nurse, I pray.'
'God knows how gladly, only say it . . .'
'Then bid your grandson – don't delay it –
Carry this letter secretly
To O . . . our neighbour. Oh, but he
Must breathe no word, must never mention
My name . . .' 'Yes, but to whom, my dear?
I must be growing dull, I fear,
Although indeed I paid attention.
We have so many neighbours, I
Could scarcely count them, should I try.'

'How dull-witted you are, nurse, truly!'
'The mind grows blunt as one grows old;
Age comes to all, my darling, duly.
The master had no need to scold
When I was young – a mere suggestion . . .'
'Ah, nurse, your mind is not in question.
What difference does that make to me?
It is my letter, don't you see,
My letter to Onegin.' 'Bless me,
Do not be cross because I fail
To grasp things . . . But you're growing pale;
Tanya, my dove, your looks distress me.'
'Oh, it is nothing, nurse, I know.
Be sure you have your grandson go.'

The day is done: he's not replying,
Another day: he still is dumb;
Dressed early, shadow-pale, and sighing,
She waits: when will the answer come?
Then Olga's suitor paid a visit.
'Has he forgotten us – what is it?
Where is your friend?' the hostess said.
Tatyana trembled and grew red.
'Something detained him. He intended
To come today, and without fail.
Perhaps what kept him was the mail,'
Thus Lensky his good friend defended.
Tatyana looked as though she heard
A black reproach in every word.

At dusk the samovar is gleaming
Upon the table, piping hot;
And as it hisses, gently steaming,
The vapour wreathes the china pot.
Now Olga sits before it, filling
The lustrous tea-cups, never spilling
A drop of the dark fragrant stream;
A serving-lad hands round the cream.
Apart, Tatyana can but linger
Beside the window; on the pane
She breathes again and yet again,
And in the mist her little finger
Describes in pensive tracery
The hallowed letters O and E.

But her soul aches, and nothing pleases,
Her eyes betray her with a tear.
The sudden sound of hoofs! . . . She freezes.
Now nearer! Galloping . . . and here
Is Eugene! By another portal
Tatyana leaps like nothing mortal
From porch to court, and shadow-light
She flies, she flies, nor in her flight
Looks backward; lightning-like she rushes
On past the bright parterre, the lawn,
The grove, the bridge, the lake, and on,
And fleeing, breaks the lilac-bushes,
And gains the brookside, breathing fast,
Where, on a rustic bench at last

She falls . . .

     'He's here! Eugene!' she panted;
'Oh, God, what can he think of me?'
Her anguished heart some peace was granted
By a dark hope of what might be.
Tatyana burned and shivered, asking:
'He's coming?' But in silence basking,
The country round about was still,
Save for the chorus on the hill
Where the maids sang to keep from cheating
The masters of the berry-crop.
They dared not let their voices drop:
For if they sing, they can't be eating
(A shrewd command that perfectly
Proves rustic ingenuity!).

Merrily, my laughing ones,
Maidens, come and trip it now,
Come and form a circle and
Foot it neatly on the green!
Girls, strike up a melody
Sing a song, a happy song,
Sing and bring a dashing lad
Hither to our frolic and
When he comes, ah, when he comes,
When we see him nearing us,
Fly, my darlings, run away,
Pelt the lad with cherries ripe,
Cherries and red raspberries,
Fling him currants ripe and red.
Eavesdroppers, be off, away!
Not for you our songs are sung,
Do not spy upon our games,
Come away, girls, come away!

Tatyana hears the chorus sounding,
But heedlessly; she cannot school
Her shaken heart to stop its pounding,
Or wait for her hot cheeks to cool.
But still she pants, her terror growing,
And hotter yet the blush is glowing
Upon her shamed and flaming cheeks;
Thus a poor moth imprisoned seeks
To free its wings, and frantic, pushes
Against the palm that holds it tight;
Thus a grey hare will quake with fright
Glimpsing behind the distant bushes
A crouching huntsman, ill-concealed,
And stop defenceless in the field.

At last she rose, and gently sighing
She sought the path, but as she turned,
Before her, there was no denying,
Eugene himself with eyes that burned
Stood like a threatening apparition;
As though she feared an inquisition
She halted, like one scorched by fire.
But what was further to transpire
After this unexpected meeting,
I cannot say; I've talked so long
That I am feeling far from strong;
Forgive me, then, for thus retreating.
Just now a walk would suit me best.
In time I shall relate the rest.

CHAPTER FOUR

La morale est dans la nature des choses.
NECKER

I–7

A woman's love for us increases
The less we love her, sooth to say –
She stoops, she falls, her struggling ceases;
Caught fast, she cannot get away.
Once lechery that took its pleasure
And boasted, bold beyond all measure,
And never loved where it desired,
Was all the art of love required.
In this important sport the jaded
Old monkeys of another age
Were proper people to engage;
Now Lovelace's renown is faded,
Gone with the styles we do not use,
With proud perukes and red-heeled shoes.

Who would not weary of evasion,
And of repeating platitudes,
Of holding forth with great persuasion
On themes to which none now alludes,
Of finding worn-out prejudices,
That even thirteen-year-old misses
Would scarcely call intelligent,
The subject of an argument?
Who would not tire of threats and rages,
Entreaties, vows, and foolish fears,
Deceit and gossip, rings and tears,
Of letters running to six pages,
Mammas and aunts who pry and peer,
And friendly husbands' heavy cheer?

Thus Eugene thought with melancholy.
In his first youth he was the prey
Of many a wild fit of folly
And never said his passions nay.
A pampered boy, allured by pleasure,
Then disappointed beyond measure,
Wearied by what he had desired,
By facile conquest swiftly tired,
At noisy gatherings and after,
In silence, hearing still the faint
Sad murmur of the soul's complaint,
And covering a yawn with laughter –
He killed eight years thus like a dunce –
The flower of life that blooms but once.

Allured by neither looks nor station,
His courting came to lose its zest;
Refused – he soon found consolation;
Betrayed – he took a welcome rest.
Though he pursued, the chase was palling;
Both love and malice scarce recalling,
Ladies he left he never missed.
Thus, for an evening game of whist,
A guest comes, an indifferent player;
Sits down; the game is done – he goes;
Drives home to take his night's repose,
His mood no gloomier, no gayer;
Not knowing in the morning where
When evening comes he will repair.

11

But our Onegin's heart was stricken
When Tanya's tender message came;
Its girlish fire began to quicken
A swarm of thoughts exempt from blame.
Again her pale face looms before him,
Her melancholy eyes adore him –
And as on these his fancy dwelt,
Onegin a pure rapture felt.
Perchance he briefly knew the fever
That thrilled him in the days gone by,
And yet her trust he'd not belie,
He would not play the base deceiver.
But to the garden let us race
Where Tanya met him face to face.

[95]

Two minutes passed with neither speaking,
Then he came up to her and said:
'You wrote me. There is no use seeking
To disavow it now. I read
A pure love's innocent effusion;
Your candour filled me with confusion;
I read a shy, confiding word,
And feelings, long quiescent, stirred;
I would not praise you, but sincerely
I would requite sincerity;
You may expect no less from me;
Your frank avowal touched me nearly.
Hear my confession, then, I pray,
And you shall judge me as you may.

'If I were one of those who rather
Enjoy staid domesticity,
If as a husband and a father
The kindly fates had fancied me,
Where should I seek a dearer treasure?
If for a moment I found pleasure
In cosy scenes of fireside life,
You, you alone would be my wife.
This is no rhetoric I'm using:
Finding my youthful dream come true –
All candour and all grace in you,
You are the helpmeet I'd be choosing:
A pledge of every loveliness,
And I'd be happy . . . more or less!

'I must confess, though loath to hurt you,
I was not born for happiness;
I am unworthy of your virtue;
I'd bring you nothing but distress.
My conscience speaks – pray let me finish;
My love, first warm, would soon diminish,
Killed by familiarity;
Our marriage would mean misery.
Then you will weep, but who supposes
Your grief will bring me to remorse?
I shall lose patience then, of course.
Infer, then, with what thorny roses
Hymen prepares to strew our way,
And that for many a long day.

15

'What is there more to be lamented
Than this: a household where the wife
Whose spouse has left her, discontented,
Grieves for the wretch throughout her life,
While the dull husband, fully knowing
Her worth, each year more sullen growing,
And jealous in a frigid way,
Can only curse his wedding-day!
And I am such. Was it naught better
Than that you sought, poor innocent,
When writing that intelligent,
That ardent and most charming letter?
The cruel fates have surely not
Designed for you so sad a lot!

'His days and dreams what man recovers?
Never shall I my soul renew . . .
I feel, if not indeed a lover's,
More than a brother's love for you.
Be patient, then, as with a brother:
One cherished fancy for another
A girl will more than once forego,
As every spring the saplings show
New leaves for those the tempests scatter.
So Heaven wills it. Your young soul
Will love again. But self-control,
My dear, is an important matter:
Though I was worthy your belief,
Impulsiveness may lead to grief.'

17

So Eugene preached and Tanya listened,
Scarce breathing, making no replies,
And blinded by the tears that glistened
Unheeded in her great dark eyes.
He offered her his arm. Despairing,
With drooping head and languid bearing
(Mechanically, as they say),
Tatyana took her silent way
Homeward, along the kitchen-garden;
And when they entered, arm in arm,
The company could see no harm
And nothing to remark or pardon;
For rustic freedom thus delights,
As does proud Moscow, in its rights.

In this affair our friend was tested
And behaved well, you will agree;
Thus once again he manifested
His soul's innate nobility;
Though there are people, most malicious,
Who called him everything that's vicious
And had no word for him but blame –
Both friends and foes (they're all the same).
We need the wit that nature gave us
To face our foes as all men must,
But from the ones we love and trust,
From our good friends, may Heaven save us!
These friends! 'Twas not for nothing that
They came into my mind so pat.

My meaning? Nothing. My intention
Is but to lull dark thoughts to sleep.
But *in parentheses* I mention
That there's no calumny so deep,
Born of a liar in the attic,
There is no notion so erratic,
No fancy of a wordly mob,
No coarse *mot* of a witty snob,
That will not be ten times repeated
To decent folk, and with a smile,
By your good friend, all without guile,
And not a single word deleted;
But he's your stay through thick and thin,
He loves you . . . as if you were kin!

H'm, h'm! dear reader, pray apprise me,
Are all your relatives quite well?
You might be pleased – if so, advise me –
To have your humble servant tell
What the word *relatives* embraces.
It means the people to whose faces
We show at all times due respect,
And whom we kiss as they expect,
And visit at the Christmas season,
Unless indeed we send a card
In token of our warm regard,
Lest they should miss us beyond reason
All during the ensuing year.
And so God grant them health and cheer!

If friends and kin are undeserving,
You may rely upon the fair,
And firmly count upon preserving
Their love, though tempests fill the air.
Oh, yes. But there's the whirl of fashion,
And then the wayward course of passion,
And the opinion of the town . . .
The sex, of course, is light as down.
And while a husband is respected
By any wife who's virtuous,
By words and looks insidious
The faithful one is soon affected:
For woman is a tender fool,
And love is but the devil's tool.

On whom shall we bestow affection,
And whom shall we confide in, pray?
In whom discover no defection?
Who will assent to all we say?
Who will not seek our faults to flout us?
Who will not spread vile lies about us?
Who will not weary us, with speed?
Who will supply our every need?
It is a phantom you are chasing,
And vainer labour there is none –
Love your own self and so have done!
This estimable friend embracing,
You prove you know, beyond a doubt,
Dear reader, what you are about.

What of the tryst, then, so ill-fated?
Alas, it is not hard to guess!
The pains of love still agitated
The soul so shy of happiness;
The promise of her spring was blighted,
But love grew greater, unrequited;
She could but peak and pine and weep,
And night would find her far from sleep.
Lost like a muted sound and vanished,
Her virgin calm is of the past;
Poor Tanya's youth is fading fast,
And health and hope and joy are banished:
Thus darkly drives the storm that shrouds
The blithest dawn in sullen clouds.

Tatyana's bloom is all but faded;
She sighs, she pines both day and night!
And all distraction finds her jaded,
She looks on nothing with delight.
The neighbours' heads and tongues are wagging:
'High time she wed!' But I am dragging
My story out, and it is wrong
To dwell on sorry things so long.
Now let me speak of something jolly,
Portraying happy love for you;
Yet bidding the poor girl adieu,
I am assailed by melancholy;
Forgive me: Tanya, from the start,
Has held the first place in my heart.

From hour to hour yet more enraptured
By the young Olga's winning ways,
Vladimir was completely captured
And found his chains a thing to praise.
Always together, now they're sitting
In her room while the light is flitting;
Or in the morning, arm in arm,
The two explore the garden's charm.
And think of it! So timid is he,
That only once in a great while,
Emboldened by his Olga's smile,
And with love's sweet confusion dizzy,
He dares to trifle with a tress
Or kiss the hem of her dear dress.

Sometimes he reads to Olga, trying
To choose such moral tales as might
Have passages on nature vying
With those Chateaubriand could write;
And certain pages (fabrications,
A snare to maids' imaginations)
He passes over in a rush
And not without a tell-tale blush.
At whiles, upon their elbows leaning,
In grave seclusion as is fit,
Above the chess-board they will sit,
And ponder each move's secret meaning,
Till Lensky, too absorbed to look,
With his own pawn takes his own rook.

If he goes home, his dreams still linger
About his Olga; it may be,
Having her album there to finger,
He decorates it earnestly:
In ink or colours he is sketching
A rustic view that she found fetching,
A tomb, a temple vowed to love,
A lyre that bears a little dove;
Or on the sheet another wrote on,
A sweet remembrance to ensure,
Below that other's signature
He writes a verse for her to dote on –
A passing thought's enduring trace
That time and change may not erase.

Of course you've often seen that treasure,
The album of a country miss,
Scrawled over by her friends at leisure
With blotted rhyme and criss-cross kiss –
Where spelling has been sadly spited,
And an eternal friendship plighted
In hacked as well as hackneyed verse
That could not very well be worse.
On the first page there's this confection:
'*Qu'écrirez-vous sur ces tablettes?*'
Beneath it: '*t. à. v.* Annette';
And on the last page this reflection:
'You are the one that I adore,
Who love you more may write yet more.'

Here you will find as decoration
Two hearts, a torch, and flow'rs, be sure,
And many a solemn protestation
Of loves that *to the grave* endure;
But for my part I do not mind
Inscribing albums of this kind:
I know there'll be a warm reception
Of any nonsense I set down,
And critics later, with a frown,
Or else a smile that's pure deception,
Will not debate and ponder it,
And search my nonsense for some wit.

But you, chance volumes that in Hades
Once graced the devil's own abode,
You tomes wherewith resplendent ladies
Torment the rhymesters *à la mode*,
You handsome albums decorated
By what Tolstoy's fine brush created,
Or graced by Baratynsky's pen,
May Heaven blast your page, amen!
When a fine lady seeks to win me
Her well-bound quarto to inscribe,
I fain would write a diatribe –
A mocking demon stirs within me
And prompts something satirical;
But they demand a madrigal!

No smart conceits does Lensky fashion
For Olga's album – not a bit!
His lyrics breathe a candid passion,
There is no sparkle here of wit;
Dear Olga is his only matter,
Her looks, her words – he does not flatter,
But with the living truth aglow,
His verses like a river flow.
Thus you, Yazykov, when affection
For God knows whom inspired your soul,
Let the sonorous stanzas roll;
And your remarkable collection
Of elegies at some far date
Will tell the story of your fate.

But hush! Our sternest critic rises
And bids us cast away the wreath
Of elegy that he despises,
And throws this challenge in our teeth:
'Stop crying, stop this tiresome quacking
  About the self-same thing, this clacking
  About the past, what's done and gone;
  Enough, sing other tunes, move on!'
'Correct; you'll bring for our inspection
  The classic trumpet, sword, and mask;
  You'll bid us free, to speed our task,
  The frozen funds of intellection –
  Eh, friend?' But no, attend again:
'Write odes, odes only, gentlemen,

'As in the old days poets wrote them –
  That ancient glory still shines bright . . .'
'What! only solemn odes? Just quote them:
  They're duller than the things we write.
  Recall Dmitriyev's castigation;
  Why should you have such veneration
  For all that musty rhetoric,
  While our sad rhymesters earn a kick?'
'Ah, but the elegy, once regnant,
  Is thin and petty, while the ode
  Travels how different a road –
  Its aim is high, its meaning pregnant . . .'
I'll not debate the point. Ye gods!
Why set two ages thus at odds?

Admiring glory, loving freedom,
Vladimir too had odes to write,
But seeing Olga wouldn't read 'em,
The lovelorn boy ignored them quite.
Lives there a poet who rehearses
To his dear charmer his own verses?
They say that life does not afford
A more magnificent reward.
How blessed the lover who is granted
The chance to read his modest songs
To her to whom his heart belongs,
And watch her, languidly enchanted!
How blessed, indeed . . . though she might choose
Something more certain to amuse.

The things that I concoct in lonely
Long hours, the melodies I mend,
I read not to the crowd, but only
To my old nurse, my childhood's friend;
Or after dinner I may vary
The boredom: nabbing the unwary
Good neighbour who's dropped in on me,
I choke him with a tragedy;
Or else (joking aside) while strolling
Beside my quiet lake, beset
By tiresome rhymes and vain regret,
I frighten the wild ducks by rolling
My tuneful stanzas forth till they
Take off, and smoothly soar away.

And now what of Onegin? Truly
I fear, friends, lest your patience fail:
His daily occupations duly
I shall, to pleasure you, detail.
As hermits live who hope for heaven
He lived – in summer rose at seven;
Clad lightly, though the air was chill,
Walked to the stream below the hill;
Gulnare's bold singer emulating,
He swam this Hellespont anew,
Then dipped into some vile review,
Keeping his morning coffee waiting,
And next he dressed . . .

A book, in shady woods a flowing
Brook, and deep sleep, the pulses' stir:
A dark-eyed, white-skinned girl, bestowing
A fresh young kiss, without demur.
A lively horse, but not too restive,
A dinner that was rather festive,
Therewith a bottle of light wine,
And solitude – this was, in fine,
Onegin's cloistral life; unheeding,
He let the summer season fly,
Nor reckoned days as they went by,
No other entertainment needing,
Forgetting friends and city ways
And wearisome planned holidays.

40

Our northern summer, swiftly flying,
Is southern winter's travesty;
And even as we are denying
Its passage, it has ceased to be.
More often now the sun was clouded;
The sky breathed autumn, sombre, shrouded;
Shorter and shorter grew the days;
Sad murmurs filled the woodland ways
As the dark coverts were denuded;
Now southward swept the caravan
Of the wild geese, a noisy clan;
And mists above the meadows brooded;
A tedious season they await
Who hear November at the gate.

41

The hazy dawn commences coldly,
The silent fields, abandoned, wait;
The hungry wolf is loping boldly
Along the highway with his mate.
The horse who scents them snorts and quivers,
The traveller, faint-hearted, shivers
And dashes uphill and is gone.
Now from the shed at crack of dawn
The herd no longer drives his cattle,
Nor calls them, noons, for mustering.
Indoors, the maid will softly sing
Above the spinning wheel's low rattle;
Her work the crackling matchwood lights,
The friend of wintry cottage nights.

42

The frosts begin to snap, and gleaming
With silver hoar, the meadows lie . . .
(The reader waits the rhyme-word: beaming,
Well, take it, since you are so sly!).
The icy river shows a burnish
That fine parquet can never furnish,
And on their skates the merry boys
Now cut the ice with scraping noise;
Down to the water's edge there stumbles
A clumsy goose, and thinks to put
Into the stream her red-webbed foot,
But stepping forth she slips and tumbles;
The first gay snowflakes spin once more
And drop in stars upon the shore.

43

What, in the country, when it's dreary,
Can a man do? Go walking there?
This is the season eyes grow weary,
Beholding bareness everywhere.
On the bleak steppe go horseback-riding?
Yes, but your horse will soon be sliding,
His worn shoe slipping on the ice,
And he will throw you in a trice.
Stay indoors, by a book befriended?
Here's Pradt and Scott. You do not think
You care to? Check accounts, or drink,
Till somehow the long evening's ended,
And so the morrow passes, too –
Your winter is cut out for you.

Onegin, like Childe Harold, scorning
All labour, took to pensive ways;
An icy bath begins his morning,
And then at home all day he stays
Alone, and sunk in calculation,
He finds sufficient occupation
In billiards, with a good blunt cue
And ivory balls, not more than two.
But as the rural dusk advances,
The game he can at last forget;
Beside the fire a table's set,
He waits; and up a troika prances,
His roans bring Lensky to the door;
Come, it is time to dine once more.

The pail is brought, the ice is clinking
Round old Moët or Veuve Clicquot;
This is what poets should be drinking
And they delight to see it flow.
Like Hippocrene it sparkles brightly,
The golden bubbles rising lightly
(The image, why, of this and that:
I quote myself, and do it pat).
I could not see it without gloating,
And once I gave my meagre all
To get it, friends, do you recall?
How many follies then were floating
Upon the magic of that stream –
What verse, what talk, how fair a dream!

But this bright sibilant potation
Betrays my stomach, and although
I love it still, at the dictation
Of prudence now I drink Bordeaux.
Aÿ is risky, if delicious;
It's like a mistress, gay, capricious,
Enchanting, sparkling, frivolous,
And empty – so it seems to us . . .
But you, Bordeaux, I always treasure
As a good comrade, one who shares
Our sorrows and our smaller cares,
And also our calm hours of leisure,
One whose warm kindness has no end –
Long live Bordeaux, the faithful friend!

The fire is out; the ashes, shifting,
Have dimmed the golden coal; half-seen,
A thread of smoke is upward drifting;
The hearth breathes warmth, and all's serene;
Up through the flue the pipe-smoke passes;
Upon the table gleam the glasses,
Their rapid bubbles hissing still;
The shadows creep across the sill.
(A friendly glass, and friendly chatter
I've always thought well suited to
The hour called '*entre chien et loup*,'
The reason doesn't really matter.)
But let us rather now inquire
What's said beside the fading fire.

'Well, how are the young ladies faring?
Your Olga? And Tatyana too?'
'Pour me a little more, be sparing . . .
Hold on, old fellow, that will do . . .
The family is well; they send you
Regards. But Olga, oh, my friend, you
Should see how lovely she has grown!
Such shoulders I have never known!
And what a throat! And what a spirit! . . .
Let's call some time. Take my advice;
You looked in at the house just twice
And never after that went near it.
But I'm a dunce! They bade me say
You are to come, and named the day.'

'I?' 'Yes, a birthday celebration –
Tatyana's – comes next Saturday.
You have her mother's invitation
And Olenka's. Why say them nay?'
'Oh, there will be a dreadful babble,
And such a crowd, a perfect rabble . . .'
'No, nobody! You're quite secure,
Only the family, I'm sure.
Oblige me! Is it such hard labour?'
'Agreed.' 'Now that is good of you!'
He said, and found his words the cue
To drink a toast to his fair neighbour,
Then fell again to talking of
His precious Olga: such is love!

The day was set, his heart elated;
When but a fortnight more had fled
He'd greet the hour so long awaited,
The secrets of the nuptial bed;
And dreaming of his exultation
He never thought of the vexation
That Hymen brings, the grief and pain,
And the cool yawns that come amain.
While we, with married life not smitten,
Are certain that it only means
A series of fatiguing scenes,
Such stuff as Lafontaine has written . . .
Ah, my poor Lensky, he was made
For such a life, I am afraid.

Beloved . . . or such was his conviction,
He was in bliss. Indeed, thrice blessed
Is he who can believe a fiction,
Who, lulling reason, comes to rest
In the soft luxury of feeling,
Like a poor sot to shelter reeling
Or (since it's ugly to be drunk)
An insect in a flower sunk;
But wretched is the man who never
Can be surprised, whose view is dim
Of word or gesture strange to him,
Who cannot feel: he is too clever,
Whose heart experience has chilled,
Whose raptures are forever stilled.

CHAPTER FIVE

Be thou spared these fearful dreams,
Thou, my sweet Svetlana.
ZHUKOVSKY

I

That year was extraordinary,
The autumn seemed so loath to go;
Upon the third of January,
At last, by night, arrived the snow.
Tatyana, still an early riser,
Found a white picture to surprise her:
The courtyard white, a white parterre,
The roofs, the fence, all moulded fair;
The frost-work o'er the panes was twining;
The trees in wintry silver gleamed;
And in the court gay magpies screamed;
While winter's carpet, softly shining,
Upon the distant hills lay light,
And all she looked on glistened white.

Here's winter! . . . The exultant peasant
Upon his sledge tries out the road;
His mare scents snow upon the pleasant
Keen air, and trots without a goad;
The bold *kibitka* swiftly traces
Two fluffy furrows as it races;
The driver on his box we note
With his red belt and sheepskin coat.
A serf-boy takes his dog out sleighing,
Himself transformed into a horse;
One finger's frostbitten, of course,
But nothing hurts when you are playing;
And at the window, not too grim,
His mother stands and threatens him.

3

Such vulgar scenes as these despising,
You may dismiss them as unfit
For verse – it would not be surprising,
There's little here that's exquisite.
Another, at a god's dictation,
Described with frenzied inspiration
First snow, and delicately wrote
Of wintry pleasures; you will dote
Upon those lines of his commending
The glories of these frosty days,
Like secret drives in cosy sleighs;
But I, my friend, am not contending
With you, nor yet with you who spin
Fine tales about your fair young Finn.

Tanya, though she could give no reason,
Was yet a thorough Russian; hence
She loved the Russian winter season
And its cold white magnificence:
The hoar-frost in the sun a-shimmer,
And sleighing, and, when light grew dimmer,
The snows still gleaming softly pink,
And the long evenings black as ink.
Yuletide they duly celebrated
As custom bade: with charm and spell
The maids would gleefully foretell
To the young ladies what was fated,
And promised them each year again
A soldier spouse and a campaign.

Tanya with simple faith defended
The people's lore of days gone by;
She knew what dreams and cards portended,
And what the moon might signify.
She quaked at omens, all around her
Were signs and warnings to confound her –
Her heart assailed, where'er she went,
By some obscure presentiment.
Puss, purring on the stove, elected
To wash his face with dainty paw,
And consequently Tanya saw
At once that guests might be expected.
If on the left she would espy
A slender crescent riding high,

6

Her face would pale, her body quivered.
And when a star dropped down the sky
And into golden fragments shivered,
She'd watch its flight with anxious eye,
And hurriedly before it perished
Confide to it the wish she cherished.
If she encountered, unaware,
A black-frocked monk, or if a hare
Should cross her path, her courage failed her,
And she went stumbling down the road,
In dread of what this might forebode;
A thousand nameless fears assailed her,
And terror-stricken she would wait
The blow of a malignant fate.

7

And yet she found it no affliction –
Her terror held a secret charm:
Since nature, fond of contradiction,
Allows a zest to our alarm.
Now Yule-tide brings its fun and folly.
The young tell fortunes, all are jolly,
For carefree youth knows no regret,
Life's vista gleams before it yet.
The aged, at the grave's grim portal,
Through spectacles, with failing eyes,
Tell fortunes, too, but otherwise:
The joys they knew have all proved mortal.
No matter: lisping like a child,
Hope lies to them, and they're beguiled.

Tatyana stares in fascination,
Seeing the molten wax assume
A shape wherein imagination
Prefigures joy to come, or doom;
Now from the dish where they are lying
The rings are plucked; each maiden, sighing,
Seeks omens in the song they sing;
This ditty sounds for Tanya's ring:
'There peasants, rich beyond all measure,
Can shovel silver with a spade;
We sing about a lucky maid,
For glory will be hers, and treasure!'
The plaintive tune, though, threatens her;
Pussy is what the girls prefer.

A frosty night; the heavens muster
A starry host of choiring spheres
That shine with a harmonious lustre . . .
Tatyana in the court appears,
And, careless of the cold, is training
A mirror on the moon, now waning;
The image trembling in the glass
Is but the wistful moon's, alas!
The crunch of snow . . . a step approaches;
Straight to the stranger Tanya speeds,
Her tender voice is like a reed's,
And rash the question that she broaches:
'Your name is – what?' He passes on,
But first he answers: 'Agafon.'

Tanya prepared for fortune-telling
As her good nurse would have her do:
And in the bath-house, not the dwelling,
They set a table laid for two;
But she took fright, our shy Tatyana;
I, too, recalling poor Svetlana,
As suddenly grew timorous,
So fortune-telling's not for us.
Tanya, her silken belt untying,
Undressed at last and went to bed.
Sweet Lel now hovers o'er her head,
And one may find a mirror lying
Beneath her pillow. Darkness keeps
All secrets safe. Tatyana sleeps.

She dreams. And wonders are appearing
Before her now, without a doubt:
She walks across a snowy clearing,
There's gloom and darkness all about;
Amid the snowdrifts, seething, roaring,
A torrent grey with foam is pouring;
Darkly it rushes on amain,
A thing the winter could not chain;
By a slim icicle united,
Two slender boughs are flung across
The waters, where they boil and toss;
And by this shaking bridge affrighted,
The helpless girl can do no more
Than halt bewildered on the shore.

She chides the waters that impede her,
But naught avails her girlish wrath;
No helping hand is near to lead her
Across in safety to the path;
A snowdrift stirs, it falls asunder:
Just fancy who appears from under!
A shaggy bear! At Tanya's cry
The creature bellows in reply
As his repellent aid he proffers;
The frightened maiden gathers strength
And puts her little hand at length
Upon the sharp-clawed paw he offers,
And steps across; her blood congeals:
The bear is marching at her heels.

Look back she dare not: fear would blind her;
She hurries, but the dreadful shape
Of her rough lackey is behind her,
In vain she struggles to escape;
Forward, with groan and grunt he lunges,
And into the deep forest plunges;
In still and sombre beauty stand
The pines, their boughs on every hand
Tufted with snow; the stars are shining
Through lofty tree-tops everywhere;
Birch, linden, aspen, all are bare;
The road is lost and past divining,
The rapids and the underbrush
Deep drifted in the snowy hush.

Into the woods, pursued, she presses;
The snow is reaching to her knee;
A branch leans down to snare her tresses,
To scratch her neck, and stubbornly
Plucks at the ear-rings she is wearing,
The trinkets rudely from her tearing;
Her small wet slipper's next to go,
All covered with the brittle snow;
She drops her handkerchief, and shivers,
Afraid to stop: the bear is near;
She dare not lift, for shame and fear,
Her trailing skirt, with hand that quivers;
She runs, he follows on and on;
She can no more, her strength is gone.

She falls into the snow; alertly
The shaggy monster seizes her,
And in his arms she lies inertly,
She does not breathe, she does not stir;
Along the forest path he crashes,
And to a humble cottage dashes:
Crowding, the trees about it grow,
And it is weighted down with snow;
One window glimmers bright and rosy,
Within, a noisy clatter swells;
The bear says: 'Here my gossip dwells,
Come warm yourself where it is cosy;'
And doing with her as he will,
He lays her down upon the sill.

Recovered, Tanya, pale and shrinking,
Looks round: the bear is gone, at least;
She hears wild shouts and glasses clinking
As at a mighty funeral feast;
The noise is queer and terrifying.
With caution through the key-hole spying
She sees . . . Why, who would credit it?
About the table monsters sit!
One is a horned and dog-faced creature,
One has a cock's head plain to see,
And there's a witch with a goatee,
A dwarf, whose tail is quite a feature,
A haughty skeleton, and that
Is half a crane and half a cat.

More horrors: here a crayfish riding
A spider; here a red-capped skull
A goose's snaky neck bestriding –
Most fearful and most wonderful!
A windmill all alone is whirling,
Its wings with crazy motions twirling;
They bark and whistle, sing and screech,
To horse's stamp and human speech!
And in the crowd that filled the hovel,
Aghast, Tatyana recognized
The dreaded one, the dearly prized:
The very hero of our novel!
Onegin sits and drinks a health,
And glances at the door by stealth.

His slightest move is overawing;
He drinks – with greedy howls they swill;
He laughs, and they are all guffawing;
He frowns, and everyone is still;
It's plain that here he is the master.
No longer fearful of disaster,
But curious, as maidens are,
Tatyana sets the door ajar . . .
A sudden gust of wind surprises
The crowd of house-sprites, blowing out
The lights, bewildering the rout;
With flashing eyes Onegin rises
And scrapes his chair along the floor;
All rise; he marches to the door.

Consumed with terror, Tanya, quaking,
Would fly the place: she cannot stir;
For all the efforts she is making,
No single sound escapes from her;
Eugene flings wide the door: defenceless,
The poor girl stands there, almost senseless;
She hears the raucous laughter swell
And sees the gaping fiends of hell:
The horns and hoofs, the whiskered faces,
The tails and tusks and bloody jaws,
The crooked trunks, the gleaming claws,
The bony hands, the sly grimaces;
All point to her, and all combine
In shouting fiercely: 'Mine! She's mine!'

'She's mine!' cries Eugene, stern and daring;
They vanish, claimed by the unknown;
The chilly dark the girl is sharing
With Eugene, and with him alone.
His gentle touch nowise dismays her,
As on a shaky bench he lays her,
And on her shoulder leans his head;
When suddenly they're visited
By Lensky and his love; light flashes;
Eugene berates them, rolls his eyes,
And lifts his hand as who defies
Unbidden guests; the scene abashes
Tatyana, and with failing breath,
The maiden lies there, pale as death.

The quarrel grows; Onegin quickly
Leaps for a knife, and Lensky falls;
The fearful shadows gather thickly;
A horrid shout assails the walls
And leaves the little hovel shaking . . .
Tatyana, terror-struck, is waking . . .
Her dear familiar room shows plain,
And through the frosty window-pane
The dawn shines ruddy; Olga rushes
In to her sister, swallow-light;
Her rosy cheeks are not less bright
Than in the north Aurora's blushes.
'Tell me your dream,' all breathlessly
She cries: 'Whom, Tanya, did you see?'

But, every interruption spurning,
She lies as though she has not heard,
Her book in hand, and slowly turning
Page after page, says not a word.
Although her book has no pretensions
To holding poets' sweet inventions,
Deep truths, or well-drawn scenes – yet not
Racine or Virgil, Walter Scott,
Or Seneca's, or Byron's pages,
Or Fashion Journal, could enthrall
As did this author: chief of all
Diviners and Chaldean sages.
This Martin Zadeka, it seems,
Was *the* interpreter of dreams.

It happened that a peddler tendered
This learned opus one fine day
To Tanya, and therewith surrendered
A prize that chanced to come his way:
Malvine – because the set was broken
Three-fifty was the price bespoken,
And in exchange he took as well
Volume the third of Marmontel,
Two Petriads, and a collection
Of fables, and a grammar too.
She thumbed her Martin till he knew
No rival in the girl's affection ...
He offered solace and delight,
And slept beside her every night.

The dream alarms her, and not knowing
What hidden meaning in it lies,
She searches for a passage showing
What such a nightmare signifies.
Some clue the index may afford her,
Where, set in alphabetic order,
She finds: abyss, ape, bear, bridge, cave,
Dirk, door, eclipse, fir, ghost, ice, knave,
Etcetera. The glosses vex her,
Her growing doubts they cannot still.
She fears the dream bodes only ill,
And yet the auguries perplex her.
The dream pervades her mournful moods,
And so for days poor Tanya broods.

But lo! from out the morning valley
The rosy dawn brings forth the sun,
And with good cheer and merry sally
The name-day feast is soon begun.
The guests are early in arriving,
Whole families of neighbours driving
Up to the steps, in coach and shay,
Calash, kibitka, crowded sleigh.
The hall is packed to suffocation,
The parlour's crowded; barking pugs,
And girls who kiss with laughs and hugs,
Increase the din of celebration;
Guests bow and scrape within the door
And nurses scream and children roar.

Beside his wife, that chubby charmer,
Plump Pustyakov strides heavily;
Here comes Gvozdin, a first-rate farmer
Whose peasants live in beggary;
The two Skotinins, grey as sages,
Line up with children of all ages:
From two to thirty, in a row;
Here's Petushkov, a rural beau;
My cousin, sleepy-eyed Buyanov,
Fluff in his hair, with visored cap
(I'm certain that you know the chap);
The old fat counsellor, Flyanov,
A gossip, glutton, clown, and cheat,
Who likes a bribe as much as meat.

Among the crush of people passes,
Leading his offspring, Kharlikov;
With them, a red-wigged man in glasses:
The wit Triquet, late of Tambov.
His pocket burns: it holds a treasure,
A song he brings for Tanya's pleasure.
All children know the melody:
Réveillez-vous, belle endormie.
The verses came – but who would know it? –
From a moth-eaten almanac;
He rescued them, and with the knack
That argues a resourceful poet,
Eliminated *belle Nina*,
Inserting: *belle Tatiana.*

Behold! from town arrives – what rapture!
The company commander, whom
Each rural mother hopes to capture,
The idol of all maids in bloom.
His news sets girlish hearts to drumming:
A regimental band is coming!
The colonel's sending it. A ball!
Upon each other's necks they fall,
Anticipating this distraction.
But dinner's served, and arm in arm
The couples to the table swarm;
Tanya's the centre of attraction.
They cross themselves, their heads incline,
Then buzzing, all sit down to dine.

Awhile all conversation ceases;
They chew. The pleasant prandial chink
Of plates and silverware increases,
The touching glasses chime and clink.
The feast goes on, but soon thereafter
The room grows loud with talk and laughter
And none can hear his neighbour speak;
They chortle, argue, shout, and squeak.
And while they all are in high feather,
The door swings wide, and Lensky's here,
Onegin too. 'At last, oh, dear!'
The hostess cries. Guests squeeze together,
Move plates and chairs with ready glee,
And seat the two friends hastily.

30

They face Tatyana, who is paler
Than is the moon one sees at dawn;
With the emotions that assail her
She trembles like a hunted fawn;
Her darkening eyes she never raises;
With stormy passion's heat she blazes;
She suffocates; she scarcely hears
The two friends' greetings; and the tears
Are all but flowing; her heart flutters,
The poor thing nearly swoons; she's ill.
But now her reason and her will
Prevail. Two words she softly mutters,
And that between her teeth, to greet
These guests, and somehow keeps her seat.

31

Eugene had long abominated
High tragedy and swoons and tears,
And girlish fits of nerves he hated:
He'd suffered from such things for years.
The feast he was quite unprepared for,
'Twas not the sort of thing he cared for;
And having noted, in a pet,
That poor Tatyana was upset,
He dropped his eyes in irritation
And sulked, and swore that he would trim
His friend for thus misleading him;
Now soothed by this anticipation,
He set his mind to work with zest,
Caricaturing every guest.

[130]

Eugene was not alone in noting
Tatyana's trouble; but each eye
Was at that moment busy gloating
Upon a succulent fat pie
(Alas, too salty), and observing
A pitch-sealed bottle they were serving
As a fit sequel to the roast:
Wine of the Don, to drink a toast.
And then appeared a row of glasses,
Each long and narrow as your waist,
Zizi, that asks to be embraced;
My soul's bright crystal, what surpasses
Your charm? My verses sang your praise;
You made me drunk in other days.

Released from the damp cork, the bottle
Pops; the wine fizzes; and Triquet,
Whom silence was about to throttle,
With dignity brings forth his lay.
The gathering, affected by it
Before it's heard, is grave and quiet.
Tatyana, breathless, cannot stir;
Triquet turns, with his sheet, to her,
And sings, off key. The song is greeted
With shouts and plaudits. Tanya now
Is forced to curtsey to his bow.
Though great, the poet's not conceited,
His toast rings out the first of all,
Then he presents the madrigal.

All greeted and congratulated
Tatyana, who spoke each one fair;
Eugene, as he his turn awaited,
Observed the girl's embarrassed air,
Her sad fatigue, her helpless languor,
And pity took the place of anger.
He bowed to her without a word,
But somehow his mere look averred
Deep tenderness; perhaps he meant it,
Or else he may, deliberately,
Have played a prank in coquetry,
Or somehow couldn't quite prevent it,
But tenderness his look *did* show,
And Tanya's heart began to glow.

The chairs shoved backward scrape the flooring;
All crowd into the drawing-room
Like bees that from the hive are pouring
Into a meadow sweet with bloom.
The feast makes every move a labour
And neighbour wheezes unto neighbour.
The ladies sit beside the fire;
The girls, off by themselves, conspire;
Green tables are set up, alluring
The gamblers, worthy men and bold:
Ombre and Boston claim the old,
And more play whist, whose fame's enduring –
Games kindred in monotony,
They form a tedious family.

The whist-players are lion-hearted:
They've played eight rubbers at a stretch,
Eight times changed places since they started;
They stop because the servants fetch
The tea. I note the hour, or nearly,
By dinner, tea, and supper merely.
Off in the country we can say
What time it is with no Breguet
Except the stomach; I may mention
In passing that my stanzas speak
Of feasts and sundry foods and eke
Of corks, with much the same attention
That to such matters Homer pays,
Who's had three thousand years of praise.

But here is tea: the girls demurely
Their steaming cups have barely stirred
When sweetly through the doors and surely
Bassoon and flute at once are heard.
Because the tune is so diverting,
His cup of tea with rum deserting,
The local Paris: Petushkov,
Comes up to carry Olga off,
And Lensky – Tanya; Kharlikova,
A virgin of ripe years, accepts
Triquet; next follow two adepts:
Buyanov leads off Pustyakova;
The ballroom summons one and all,
Thus brilliantly begins the ball.

40

At the beginning of my story
I thought to paint (see Chapter One)
A northern ball in all its glory,
A thing Albani might have done;
But yielding to a dream's distraction,
I reminisced of the attraction
That ladies' feet have had for me.
Oh, I have erred sufficiently
In tracking you! I should be moving
On other paths, since youth is spent,
And grow, with time, intelligent,
My style and my affairs improving,
And, if my novel is to thrive,
Free from digressions Chapter Five.

41

Like giddy youth forever swirling
In dizzy circles round and round,
The waltz sends tireless couples twirling
To flute and viol's merry sound.
Revenge approaches, so, concealing
A smile, Onegin is appealing
To Olga. First they spin about,
Then he suggests they sit one out,
And chats of this and that politely;
A moment, and the pair once more
Are waltzing round the dancing-floor.
All wonder whether they see rightly;
And staring in dismayed surprise,
Lensky can scarcely trust his eyes.

Now the mazurka's strains are sounding.
Of old the ballroom used to shake
To the mazurka; with the pounding
Of heels the stout parquet would quake,
And window-sashes rattled loudly.
Not now: we, like the ladies, proudly
And smoothly glide on polished boards;
But the provincial town affords
A place for the old-fashioned splendour:
The leaps, the heels, the whiskers fair,
Are just the same as what they were;
The country to the past is tender,
Nor bends to fashion's tyrannies:
The modern Russian's worst disease.

43–4

My lively cousin now advancing,
Presents the charming sisters both
To Eugene, who at once goes dancing
Away with Olga, nothing loath;
He leads her, nonchalantly gliding,
And in an attitude confiding,
His head above her fondly bent,
Whispers an outworn compliment,
And presses her soft hand – elation
Inflames the girl's conceited face;
My Lensky's fury grows apace;
He waits with jealous indignation
The end of the mazurka, and
For the cotillion begs her hand.

She cannot. No? But why? She's given
Onegin the cotillion. Lord!
What does he hear? She dared . . . He's driven
To think the girl that he adored
Is but a flirt. Though she is barely
Out of her swaddling-clothes, she's fairly
Accomplished as a vile coquette!
Such treachery who could forget?
Poor Lensky cannot bear his sorrow.
He curses women's whims with force,
Goes out at once, demands his horse,
And dashes off. Before the morrow
A brace of pistols and two balls
Will square accounts, whoever falls.

CHAPTER SIX

Là sotto giorni nubilosi e brevi
Nasce una gente a cui l'morir non dole.
PETRARCH

I

Revenge was something of a pleasure,
But Eugene, now his friend was gone,
Was bored again beyond all measure;
Olenka too began to yawn,
By her dull partner's mood infected;
And as she looked about, dejected,
For Lensky, the cotillion seemed
To her a tiresome thing she dreamed.
It's over. Having supped, the gentry
Are glad at last to take a rest:
A place is found for every guest
'Twixt the maid's attic and the entry,
And gratefully to bed they creep;
Eugene alone goes home to sleep.

All's hushed: within the parlour, sighing
And snoring, heavy Pustyakov
Beside his heavy mate is lying.
Gvozdin, Buyanov, Petushkov,
And Flyanov, somewhat ill, encumber
The dining-room: on chairs they slumber.
Upon the floor Triquet we view
In flannels and a night-cap too.
The girls with Olga and Tatyana
Are settled: they are fast asleep;
But at her window, fain to weep,
Poor Tanya, lighted by Diana,
Stares out upon the shadowed lea:
There is no sleep for such as she.

Once more Tatyana's heart is drumming;
Delight is mingled with distress
As she reviews Onegin's coming
And his brief look of tenderness –
And then, with Olga, how he acted!
She puzzles till she is distracted,
And jealous longing frets the maid –
As though a chilly hand were laid
Upon her heart, as though a rumbling
Black chasm were gaping at her feet . . .
'But ruin at his hands is sweet,'
Says Tanya, 'Nay, I am not grumbling:
Complaint will make my pain no less.
He cannot give me happiness.'

4

Proceed, my tale! Here's matter for ye,
Good readers: a new face arrives.
Five versts away from Krasnogorye,
Our Lensky's village, lives and thrives,
'Mongst thinkers who are few and cloudy,
Zaretzky, once a jolly rowdy,
A gambler who won all the stakes,
A tavern tribune, chief of rakes,
But now a kind and simple father,
Albeit still a bachelor,
A good landed proprietor,
A friend in need, as you will gather –
Even a man of honour: thus
The times improve, and better us!

5

Time was when all the world was vying
In praise of his base hardihood;
He hit an ace, there's no denying,
At fifteen feet: his aim was good.
One day when leading his battalion,
He fell from off his Kalmuck stallion
Drunk as an owl, into a trench,
And so was captured by the French –
A precious gain! The man was guided
By honour's dictates, was indeed
A modern Regulus; at need
He'd suffer bonds again, provided
That at Véry's on credit he
Could drain each morning bottles three.

He well knew how to set you laughing,
Made game of fools, and being bent
On secret or on open chaffing,
Could hoodwink the intelligent;
Though on occasion like a duffer
This clever jester had to suffer,
And for the pranks he liked to play
Took punishment once in a way.
He liked debate, and sometimes rudely
And sometimes neatly made retort,
Or shrewdly held his peace; in sport
Would start a quarrel quite as shrewdly,
To have two friends at daggers drawn
And send them, armed, from bed at dawn,

Or into concord gently shame them,
To earn a luncheon from the two,
And later privately defame them
With a gay jest and words untrue.
Sed alia tempora! Such jolly
Pranks (like love's dream, another folly)
Belong to youth, with youth are fled.
And my Zaretzky, as I said,
Beneath the shade of his acacias
Has found a refuge from the blast
And lives like a true sage at last,
Plants cabbages like old Horatius,
And raises fowls, while at his knee
The children learn their A.B.C.

He was no fool; and Eugene, ready
To praise his mind if not his heart,
Admired his judgement, always steady,
And found his comments sane and smart.
He often paid a call, surmising
A welcome; it was not surprising
For Eugene to behold him there
That morning, gay and debonair.
He barely spoke; his urgent mission
Zaretzky was not one to shirk –
At once he offered with a smirk
A note of Lensky's composition;
Onegin took the letter to
The window, where he read it through.

The poet, swift in thought and action,
With most polite and cool address,
Herein demanded satisfaction,
For honour could require no less.
The messenger was not kept waiting:
Onegin without hesitating
Replied as though he little cared
What came of it: 'Always prepared.'
On hearing this, Zaretzky started
To go: he had no wish to stay,
And he was busy anyway,
And so without more words, departed;
But left alone, Onegin sighed,
With his own self dissatisfied.

And rightly: for Onegin, sitting
In judgement on himself could be
Severe, and he was not acquitting
Himself, even in privacy.
First: he accused himself of mocking
Young timid love, and that was shocking.
Second: the poet was a fool,
But at eighteen that is the rule;
And holding him in such affection
Eugene should not have been so rash,
Not thus have sought to cut a dash,
Nor shown a fighter's predilection,
But, like a man of worth and sense,
Have acted with intelligence.

Had he been quicker in revealing –.
Instead of bristling at the start –
That he was yet a man of feeling,
He'd have disarmed the youthful heart.
'Too late,' he thinks, 'And then that vicious
Old duelist can be malicious:
He thrust his nose in right away,
And he would have a deal to say . . .
Of course, one should reward his gabble
With scorn; yet smiles upon the lips
Of fools, and slyly whispered quips . . .'
Lo! the opinion of the rabble
Is honour's mainspring, I'll be bound –
The thing that makes the world go round.

The poet, with impatience burning,
Sits home, awaiting the reply;
And here Zaretzky is returning
With solemn gait and sparkling eye.
The young Othello is delighted!
He feared that he had not incited
The rogue, who somehow would escape
By a sly dodge or ready jape.
He savours the few words that settle
His doubts: for meet they surely will
At dawn tomorrow, near the mill;
Then let each man be on his mettle:
They'll cock the trigger and let fly,
Their mark the temple or the thigh.

Resolved to hate a flirt so cruel,
Now Lensky vowed he would not see
The girl at all before the duel;
He marked the time, and presently
He waved his hand, as one who'd rue it
And was at Olga's ere he knew it!
He was convinced the fickle fair
Would be dismayed to see him there;
But no! – straight down the steps to meet him
Unhesitatingly she ran,
Bewildering the wretched man,
And turned a joyful face to greet him
In the same carefree lively way
As upon any other day.

'Why did you leave,' the maiden asked him,
'So very early yesterday?'
Deeply disturbed as thus she tasked him,
Poor Lensky scarce knew what to say.
His jealousy and his vexation
Were banished by her animation,
Her look, so candid and serene,
Her sweet simplicity of mien! . . .
He gazes, and his heart is riven:
She loves him still; and in remorse,
He now repents him of the course
He took, and fain would be forgiven;
He trembles, cannot say a word,
His heart leaps up, his soul is stirred.

15–17

In Olga's presence poor Vladimir
Ignores what happened yesterday,
And full of grief the wistful dreamer
Broods over all he dare not say:
'From threatened ruin I'll retrieve her,
I shall not suffer the deceiver
To tempt with tender word and sigh
The youthful heart; I will defy
The poisonous vile worm that mumbles
The lily-stem, and withers so
The bud that just begins to blow,
But ere 'tis open, fades and crumbles.'
These proud reflections all portend:
I'll have a duel with my friend.

Had he but known the wounding sorrow
That burdened my Tatyana's heart!
Had Tanya known that on the morrow
Fresh grief would cause a keener smart –
Could she but have foreseen the meeting
And the two friends for death competing,
She then, as love has power to do,
Might have united them anew!
But none as yet came near divining
Her passion, not by chance or skill;
Eugene was apt at keeping still;
In secret Tanya was repining;
The nurse alone might well have guessed,
But she was slow of wit at best.

All evening Lensky was distracted,
A glum, and next a merry man;
But nurselings of the Muse have acted
Like this since first the world began;
With frowning brow he would be sitting
At the spinet, then swiftly quitting
The music, he would whisper low
To Olga: 'I am happy – no?'
But it is late, he should be leaving;
His heart is all but crushed with pain,
And as he says farewell again
He feels that it must break with grieving.
She looks at him in some dismay.
'What ails you?' 'Nothing.' So – away.

At home his pistols claimed attention;
He looked them over, boxed them right,
Undressed, and opened – need I mention? –
Schiller, of course, by candle-light.
But ever sadder, ever fonder,
He has a single thought to ponder:
He seems to see his Olga there
Unutterably dear and fair.
Inspired by tender melancholy,
Vladimir shuts the book, and then
There pours in torrents from his pen
Verse full of amatory folly,
Which he declaims with ecstasy
Like Delwig drunk in company.

By chance, these verses have not perished;
I have them here for you to see:
'Oh, golden days, my springtide cherished,
Ah, whither, whither did you flee?
The day to come, what is it bearing?
In vain into the darkness staring
I try to glimpse it; but I trust
The law of Fate is ever just.
From the drawn bow the arrow leaping
May pass me by or pierce me through;
Yet all is well – each has his due:
The hour for waking and for sleeping;
The day of busy cares is blest,
And blest the darkness bringing rest.

'The ray of dawn will shine tomorrow,
And day will brighten wold and wave,
When I, mayhap, past joy and sorrow,
Shall know the secrets of the grave,
And Lethe's sluggish tide will swallow
The poet, and the world will follow
His course no more; but, oh, most dear,
Will you not come to shed a tear
Upon the urn, and think: "Ill-fated!
He loved me, and the dawn of life
With its unseasonable strife
To me alone he dedicated!..."?
Dear friend, before this heart is numb –
Your spouse awaits; come to me, come!...'

His strain was languid, dark (romantic,
We call it – if no trace I find
Of such a manner, I'm pedantic,
And how it strikes me, never mind).
The poet did not think of stopping
Until, near dawn, his head was dropping
Upon 'ideal' – modish word –
And sleep at last her boon conferred;
But scarce did consciousness forsake him
When into the hushed study came
His neighbour, calling out his name,
Not hesitating to awake him.
'Get up,' he cried, 'Past six, I vow
Onegin's waiting for us now.'

He erred; for Eugene, hardy sinner,
Was sleeping, heedless of the clock;
The shades of night are growing thinner,
And Lucifer's hailed by the cock;
Onegin sleeps and does not worry.
The sun appears, a brief snow-flurry
Is gaily whirling overhead,
And still our Eugene lies abed
In cosy comfort, sleeping sweetly.
At last he rouses, opens wide
His drowsy eyes, and draws aside
The bed-curtains; awake completely,
He marks the hour with some dismay:
He must be off without delay.

Responding to his hasty ringing,
In runs his valet, prompt Guillot,
His dressing-gown and slippers bringing,
And hands him linen white as snow.
With utmost speed Onegin dresses,
And bids his servant, since time presses,
Prepare with him to leave the place
At once, and bear the weapon-case.
The sledge awaits. He does not tarry:
He's in, and flying to the mill.
They come. Quite unaffected still,
He gives his man the arms to carry
(Lepage's work), and has him tie
The horses to an oak nearby.

Upon the dam leaned Lensky, waiting,
The while Zaretzky with a sneer
Upon the mill-stone dissertating
Was quite the rustic engineer.
Onegin comes, apologizing.
Zaretzky, not at all disguising
Surprise, asks: 'Where's your second, pray?'
A classicist in such a fray,
And sentimentally devoted
To method, he would not allow
That one be potted anyhow,
But by rule only, and he doted
Upon the good old-fashioned ways
(A bias worthy of our praise).

'My second?' Eugene said, 'Permit me:
My worthy friend, Monsieur Guillot.
If fault there be, you will acquit me
Of making such a choice, I know;
He is, though not renowned or quoted,
An honest fellow, be it noted.'
Zaretzky bit his lip, quite vexed,
Onegin turned to Lensky next:
'Well, shall we start?' The young Othello
Responded: 'Why should we delay?'
Behind the mill they went straightway.
Zaretzky and the *honest fellow*
Went off and talked in solemn wise;
The foes stood by, with downcast eyes.

The foes! How long had they been parted
By this most black and vengeful mood?
How long since they were happy-hearted,
And sharing leisure, thoughts, and food,
And doings, in a friendly fashion?
But now, the prey of evil passion,
Like those whom an old feud besots,
As in a nightmare each one plots
In silence to destroy the other . . .
Were it not better, if before
Those gentle hands were stained with gore
Beneath a laugh their rage would smother?
But worldly quarrels breed the dread
Of worldly scorn, and thus are fed.

The gleaming pistols are held steady
As hammers on the ramrods knock;
The bullets are crammed down already;
You hear the clicking of a cock.
Into the pan the powder's sifted,
The jagged flint still harmless, lifted.
Behind a stump among the trees
Guillot is standing, ill at ease.
Their gestures arguing decision,
The enemies their mantles doff.
And now Zaretzky measures off
Thirty-two paces with precision;
At either end the two friends stand,
Each with a weapon in his hand.

'Approach!' How calm and cold their faces,
  As the two foes, with even tread,
Not aiming yet, advance four paces,
  Four steps toward a narrow bed.
First Eugene, still advancing duly,
Begins to raise his pistol coolly.
Now five steps more the pair have made,
And Lensky, firm and unafraid,
Screws up his eye and is preparing
  To take aim also – but just then
  Onegin fires . . . Once again
Fate shows herself to be unsparing.
  The fatal hour is past recall;
  The poet lets his pistol fall,

His hand upon his breast lays lightly,
  And drops. His clouded eyes betray
Not pain, but death. Thus, sparkling whitely
  Where the quick sunbeams on it play,
A snowball down the hill goes tumbling
And sinks from sight, soon to be crumbling.
Eugene, with ice in all his veins,
Runs to the youth whose life-blood stains
The ground, looks, calls him . . . But no power
  Avails to rouse him: he is gone.
  The poet at the very dawn
Of life has perished like a flower
  That from its stem a gale has wrenched.
  Alas! the altar-fire is quenched.

He did not stir, but like one dreaming
He lay most strangely there at rest.
The blood from the fresh wound was streaming:
The ball had pierced clean through the breast.
A moment since, this heart was quickened
By poetry and love, or sickened
By hate and dread, and strongly beat
With dancing blood, with living heat.
But now, 'tis as a house forsaken,
Where all is silent, dark and drear,
The shutters closed, the windows blear
With chalk. No knock can ever waken
The lady of the house: she's fled –
Where to, God knows; she never said.

'Tis pleasant with a wicked sally
To make a man feel like an ass,
To see him, baited, turn and rally,
And glance, unwilling, in the glass,
Ashamed to own his every feature;
'Tis yet more pleasant if the creature
Should howl absurdly: 'It is I!'
And yet more pleasant, on the sly
To make his noble coffin ready:
A proper distance to allow,
Then, aiming at his pallid brow,
To hold the pistol straight and steady;
But yet the pleasure's dulled if he
Is launched into eternity.

Suppose your pistol-shot has ended
A comrade's promising career,
One who, by a rash glance offended,
Or by an accidental sneer,
During a drunken conversation
Or in a fit of blind vexation
Was bold enough to challenge you –
Will not your soul be filled with rue
When on the ground you see him, stricken,
Upon his brow the mark of death,
And watch the failing of his breath,
And know that heart will never quicken?
Say, now, my friend, what will you feel
When he lies deaf to your appeal?

Onegin grips his pistol tightly,
His heart with sore repentance filled,
Beholding Lensky. 'Well?' Forthrightly
The neighbour now declares: 'He's killed.'
He's killed! The fearful affirmation
Makes Eugene quake with consternation.
He calls for help, in misery;
And in the sleigh most carefully
The frozen corpse Zaretzky places,
To take the awful cargo home.
The horses scent the dead, and foam
Is slobbered over bit and traces,
As, sped like arrows from the bow,
They snort and gallop o'er the snow.

Friends, for the poet you are grieving:
Cut off before his hopes could bloom;
The world of glory thus bereaving,
He came, unripe, unto the tomb!
Where is the burning agitation,
Where is the noble aspiration,
The thoughts of youth so high and grave,
The tender feelings and the brave?
Where are the storms of love and longing,
The thirst for knowledge, toil, and fame,
The dread of vice, the fear of shame,
And you, bright phantoms round him thronging,
You, figments of sweet reverie,
You, dreams of sacred poesy?

Mayhap he would have been reputed,
Or gloriously served the world;
Mayhap the lyre so early muted
Beneath his fingers would have hurled
A mighty music down the ages.
Perchance he would have earned the wages
By worldly approbation paid.
Or it may be his martyred shade
Bore to the grave to sleep forever
A holy secret, and a voice
To make the soul of man rejoice
Is lost to us, and he will never
Beyond the grave thrill with amaze
To hear a people's hymn of praise.

Perchance a humble lot awaited
The poet, and he may, forsooth,
Like many others have been fated
To lose his ardour with his youth.
He might have altered and deserted
The Muse – to marriage been converted,
And worn in comfort, far from town,
Horns and a quilted dressing-gown;
He might have learned that life was shabby
At bottom, and, too bored to think,
Have been content to eat and drink,
Had gout at forty, fat and flabby;
He might have gone to bed and died
While doctors hemmed and women cried.

40

What'er was to befall Vladimir,
One thought must fill your heart with pain:
The lover, poet, pensive dreamer,
Alas! by a friend's hand was slain.
There is the spot if you would know it:
Left of the village where the poet
Once dwelt, two pines are intertwined –
Below you see the river wind
That waters well the nearby valley.
The women mowing oft repair
To plunge their tinkling pitchers there,
And there the weary ploughmen dally.
Beside that stream with shadows laced
A simple monument is placed.

[155]

Near by (when springtime rains have peppered
The fields with droplets once again),
Weaving his shoe of bast, the shepherd
Sings of the Volga fishermen;
And the young city miss who's facing
A summer in the country, racing
Across the meadowland alone,
Will halt her horse beside the stone,
Tug at the leather rein, and turning
Her gauzy veil aside to see
The simple lines there graven, she
Will feel her heart with pity burning,
And as she reads, the tears will rise
To mist her wide and tender eyes.

And plunged in sorry thought, more slowly
On through the field the girl will ride,
The while her wistful spirit wholly
With Lensky's fate is occupied;
'And what of Olga?' is her query:
'Was all her life thereafter dreary?
Or was the time of sorrow brief?
Where did her sister take her grief?
Where is the saturnine betrayer,
The smart coquettes' smart enemy,
The exile from society
Who was the fair young poet's slayer?'
In time, my readers, you shall hear
It all, in detail, never fear,

Not now. I love my hero truly,
And shall return to him, I vow,
All his concerns recounting duly,
But that is not my pleasure now.
The years to rugged prose constrain me,
No more can hoyden rhymes detain me,
And I admit, in penitence,
I court the Muse with indolence.
No more I find it quite so pressing
To soil the sheets with flying quill;
But other fancies, bleak and chill,
And other cares, severe, distressing,
In festive crowds, in solitude,
Upon my dreaming soul intrude.

By new desires I am enchanted,
New sorrows come, my heart to fret;
The hopes of old will not be granted,
The olden sorrows I regret.
Ah, dreams! where has your sweetness vanished?
Where's youth (the rhyme comes glibly) banished
And is the vernal crown of youth
Quite withered now in very truth?
Can the sad thought with which I flirted
In elegiac mood at last
Be fact, and can my spring be past
(As I in jest so oft asserted)?
Will it no more return to me?
Shall I be thirty presently?

The afternoon of life is starting,
I must admit the sorry truth.
Amen: but friendly be our parting,
My frivolous and merry youth!
My thanks for all the hours of gladness,
The tender torments, and the sadness,
The storm and strife, the frequent feast;
For all your great gifts and your least,
My thanks. Alike in peace and riot
I found you good, and I attest
I tasted all your joys with zest;
Enough! My soul is calm and quiet
As on another road I fare,
Free from the loads I used to bear.

Let me look back. Farewell, you bowers
Where days would float by lazily,
Where first I yielded to the powers
Of passion and of reverie!
And you, oh, youthful inspiration,
Come, rouse anew imagination –
Upon the dull mind's slumbers break,
My little nook do not forsake;
Let not the poet's heart know capture
By sullen time, and soon grow dry
And hard and cold, and petrify
Here in the world's benumbing rapture,
This pool we bathe in, friends, this muck
In which, God help us, we are stuck.

CHAPTER SEVEN

Moscow, Russia's darling daughter,
Where's your equal to be found? DMITRIEV

How can one not love Moscow, pray? BARATYNSKY

Speak ill of Moscow! There's your traveller!
Where will you find a better place, good sir?
Oh, yes, what's far away, that we prefer! GRIBOYEDOV

I

From nearby hills the snow, already
Obeying the spring sun's commands,
Flows down in muddy streams and steady
Into the flooded meadowlands.
Still half asleep, nature is meeting
The year's bright dawn with gentle greeting.
The heavens glow with azure light.
The naked woods surprise the sight,
A delicate green down assuming.
The bee deserts her waxen cell
To gather tribute from the dell.
Soon the dry valleys will be blooming;
The cattle low; the nightingale
Has thrilled by night the silent dale.

[159]

Ah, spring, fair spring, the lovers' season,
How sad I find you! How you flood
My soul with dreams that challenge reason,
And with strange languor fill my blood!
My stricken heart cries out and fails me
When once the breath of spring assails me,
Although its touch be soft as fleece,
While I lie lapped in rural peace!
Is it that I was born to languish,
And all that sparkles, triumphs, sings,
Is alien to my breast, and brings
No gift but weariness and anguish
To one whose soul has perished, and
Who sees the dark on every hand?

3

Or is it that we fail to cherish
The tender leaves, but in the spring
Mourn those that autumn doomed to perish,
The while we hear the woodland sing?
Or are our thoughts in truth so cruel
That nature's season of renewal
But brings to mind our fading years
That no hope of renewal cheers?
Or it may be that we are taken
In our poetic reverie
Far back to a lost spring, and we,
By dreams of a far country shaken,
Recall with pain the vanished boon:
A night of magic, and a moon . . .

4

Kind drones, and you who wisely savour
Your pleasures with a taste more keen,
And you who bask in fortune's favour,
And you, skilled pupils of Levshin,
You rustic Priams, and you gentle
Fair ladies who are sentimental –
Spring calls you to the verdant soil,
To sunny gardens' fragrant toil;
The time of tempting nights approaches,
When every walk fresh wonders yields;
Then, hurry, hurry to the fields!
Have your own horses pull your coaches,
Or post-horses, if thus inclined,
But fast or slow, leave town behind!

5

And you, my reader, wise and witty,
In your imported carriage, pray
Desert at last the restless city
Where winter-long you were so gay;
And while my wanton muse rejoices
We'll listen to the forest voices,
Upon the nameless river's shore
In that same hamlet where of yore
My Eugene through the winter tarried,
An idle, cheerless recluse, near
Young Tanya, whom I still hold dear,
Poor dreamer whom he sadly harried;
But where no more one meets his face . . .
And where he left a lasting trace.

Within the hill-encircled valley
Come seek the stream that slowly goes
Through meadowland and linden alley,
On down to where the river flows.
The nightingale, this season's lover,
There sings all night; wild roses cover
The bank; one hears a gentle spring;
And where two pines their shadows fling
A gravestone tells its mournful story.
The passer-by may read it clear:
'Vladimir Lensky slumbers here,
Who early found both death and glory,
In such a year, at such an age;
Take rest, young poet, as thy wage.'

Upon a trailing branch suspended
Above this modest urn there hung
A wreath, that by the breeze befriended
Caressed the tomb o'er which it swung.
There, when the tardy moon was shining,
Two girls would come, and sadly twining
Their arms about each other, creep
To the low grave, to sit and weep.
But now . . . the tombstone and its story
Are quite forgot. The path is now
O'ergrown. No wreath hangs on the bough;
Alone the shepherd, weak and hoary,
As erstwhile comes, to hum an air
And plait his humble footgear there.

Poor Lensky! Olga's heart was laden
With sorrow, but her tears were brief.
Alas! a young and lively maiden
Can scarce be faithful to her grief.
Another captured her attention,
Another's amorous invention
Soon found a way to soothe her pain;
An uhlan wooed her, not in vain;
She loves an uhlan with devotion . . .
Already, 'neath the bridal crown,
Before the altar, head cast down,
She stands, suffused with shy emotion,
Her lowered eyes agleam the while,
And on her lips a gentle smile.

11

Poor Lensky! Past the grave's grim portal,
Was the sad singer shocked to learn
That Olga's love, alas, was mortal,
And did his shade in sorrow yearn?
Or, lulled by Lethe's quiet flowing,
And blissful still, since all unknowing,
By nothing stirred, where all is dim,
Is this world shut for aye to him?
Oblivion is waiting for us
Beyond the grave, yes, at the end
The voice of mistress, foe, and friend,
Is hushed. Alone the angry chorus
Of heirs is heard, indecently
Disputing your small legacy.

Not long the Larin house was waking
To Olga's voice: away she went,
Since now her uhlan was betaking
Himself back to his regiment.
The poor old lady, broken-hearted,
Wept o'er her daughter as they parted,
And seemed about to faint and fall;
But Tanya had no tears at all;
And yet her face was pale and clouded
As that of one beneath a spell.
When all went out to say farewell,
And round the loaded carriage crowded,
She too at length came forth, and nigh
The couple stood, to say good-bye.

As one who through a fog is peering,
Tatyana watched them drive away
Till they were out of sight and hearing. . . .
She is alone, alack-a-day!
The bosom friend on whom she doted,
Her dove, her confidante devoted,
Is snatched away from her by Fate
Who best knows how to separate.
She has no aim, no occupation,
But like a shadow moves about,
Or on the garden gazes out . . .
But nothing offers consolation,
Nor eases tears too long suppressed,
Nor soothes the ache within her breast.

Tatyana's solitude adds fuel
To her vain passion day by day;
Her heart speaks ever of the cruel
Onegin, also far away.
She will not see him, the betrayer;
Nay, she must hate her brother's slayer.
The poet is no more . . . his lot
Was to be readily forgot.
Though he was brave, though he was gifted,
His bride was soon content to be
Another's, and his memory
Like smoke across the azure drifted;
Two hearts, one may perhaps believe,
Yet grieve for him . . . But wherefore grieve?

By the still stream, with dusk descending,
The beetle droned. Loath to retire,
The dancers now were homeward wending.
On the far bank the smoky fire
Built by the fishermen was flaring.
Now through the open meadow faring,
Where moonlight silvered shrub and stone,
Tatyana, dreaming, walked alone.
She clambered up a hill, commanding
A village view she seemed to know,
A garden river-girt, and lo!
Nearby, she saw the mansion standing.
Tanya surveys it with a start,
And faster, faster throbs her heart.

A trespasser may hope for pardon.
'I am not known here. He is gone . . .
I might just see the house and garden,'
She thinks, uncertain, and goes on.
Her mind with agitation seething,
Downhill she trudges, scarcely breathing.
She looks about in puzzled sort,
And enters the deserted court.
The dogs attack her, all but biting
The stranger. At her frightened cry,
Out from the house the serf-boys fly,
A noisy brood. Not without fighting,
They chase the dogs away, alert
Lest the young lady should be hurt.

'The manor-house,' says Tanya, shyly,
'I should most dearly like to see.'
At once the children run off spryly
To ask Anisya for the key.
Anisya surely won't ignore them:
Yes, now the door is opened for them,
And Tanya enters. Here her prince,
Our hero, lived not so long since.
She looks about, with heart that flutters:
A cue rests on the table-top,
Upon the couch, a riding-crop.
She walks ahead. The old crone mutters:
'The fireplace, miss, please look at it –
'Twas here the master used to sit.

'With the late Lensky almost nightly
He dined here. What fine gentlemen!
Please follow me,' she said politely.
'Here you will find the master's den.
He took his coffee here, and rested,
The steward came here when requested;
Here, mornings, he would read his book . . .
This too was the old master's nook;
Of Sundays, putting on his glasses,
It was his pleasure quietly
To play a game of cards with me,
Beside the window. So life passes . . .
May his soul now be with the blest,
And in the grave his bones have rest!'

Tatyana thrills with pain and pleasure
At everything she gazes on;
Each object seems a priceless treasure,
Commemorating one who's gone;
She looks, half soothed and half excited,
First at the desk, with lamp unlighted,
The pile of books no longer read,
Then at the rug that decks the bed,
The haughty portrait of Lord Byron,
The view that once met Eugene's sight,
And likes the pallid evening light
That shows a statuette of iron:
The arms are crossed – a well-known pose –
The hat is cocked, the brow morose.

In the smart sanctum, all a-quiver,
Tatyana, spell-bound, lingers still.
But it is late. Above the river,
The grove's asleep. The wind blows chill.
The dale is dark and vapour-ridden.
Behind a hill the moon is hidden;
And pleasant though it is to roam,
The fair young pilgrim must go home.
Pretending calmness, Tanya quitted
The room, though not without a sigh,
And pleading first that by-and-by
She might return; yes, if permitted,
Although the house was empty, she
Would make the den her library.

She halted at the gateway, telling
The housekeeper a slow good-bye;
And came to the abandoned dwelling
Next day before the sun was high.
Into the silent study, setting
Aside all timid thoughts, forgetting
The world without, Tatyana crept,
And there she stayed, and wept, and wept.
The volumes at long last succeeding
In catching Tanya's eye, she took
A glance at many a curious book,
And all seemed dull. But soon the reading
Absorbed the girl, and she was thrown
Headlong into a world unknown.

Onegin's taste for books had vanished
Long since, but notice if you please
That there were works he never banished
From his affection; they were these:
Lord Byron's tales, which well consorted
With two or three bright-backed imported
Romances, upon every page
Exhibiting the present age,
And modern man's true soul divulging:
A creature arid, cold, and vain,
Careless of others' joy and pain,
In endless reverie indulging,
One whose embittered mind finds zest
In nothing, but can never rest.

Some pages held a sharp incentive
To reading, where a finger-nail
Had marked the place; and, more attentive,
Tatyana scanned them without fail.
She noted, trembling and excited,
What passage, what remark delighted
Onegin, what shrewd line expressed
A thought in which he acquiesced.
She found the margins most appealing:
The pencil-marks he made with care
Upon the pages everywhere
Were all unconsciously revealing:
A cross, a question-mark, a word –
From these the man might be inferred.

So Tanya bit by bit is learning
The truth, and, God be praised, can see
At last for whom her heart is yearning
By Fate's imperious decree.
A danger to all lovely ladies,
Is he from Heaven or from Hades?
This strange and sorry character,
Angel or fiend, as you prefer,
What is he? A mere imitation,
A Muscovite in Harold's cloak,
A wretched ghost, a foreign joke
But with a new interpretation,
A lexicon of snobbery
And fashion, or a parody?

Has she the answer to the riddle
And has she found *the word*? She lets
The time run on, and in the middle
Of her researches quite forgets
She should go home, where guests are waiting
And where indeed of her they're prating.
'What's to be done? She's not a child,'
The mother groans. 'It drives me wild;
I've married off my younger daughter,
Tatyana should be settled, too.
But, heavens, what am I to do
When she can only throw cold water
On every single suitor's hopes?
All day she roams the woods and mopes.'

'In love with someone?' 'But who is it?
Buyanov's hand she has refused,
And Petushkov's. We had a visit
From the hussar, Pykhtin, who used
As many wiles as I could mention
To win her – showed her such attention!
She must accept at last, I thought,
But no! the whole thing came to naught.'
'You'll have to take her to the city –
To Moscow: it's the brides' bazaar;
That's where the eligibles are!'
'Not on my income, more's the pity!'
'But for a season it will do;
If not, my dear, I'll see you through.'

By this delightful counsel guided,
The mother fell to figuring
Expenses, and therewith decided
A Moscow winter was the thing.
The news gives Tanya little pleasure.
To let the worldlings take the measure
Of her demure provincial ways,
Revealing to their haughty gaze
Her dowdy frocks, and to their mercies
Her countrified simplicity
Of speech, and earn the mockery
Of Moscow beaus and Moscow Circes!
Oh, horror! Better far to stay
Safe in the woodland, hid away.

She rises as the morning flushes
With rosy light the eastern skies,
And off into the fields she rushes,
To say, with sorrow in her eyes:
'Farewell, you dear and peaceful valleys,
Familiar hills, familiar alleys,
You woodlands where I used to roam,
Farewell, you friendly skies of home;
Kind, cheerful nature, it is bitter
To leave such quiet haunts as these
For worldly shows and vanities,
The crowd, the hubbub, and the glitter!
And why? What am I striving for?
What does my future hold in store?'

Her walks are longer, she will dally
Beside a stream, or on a hill,
And find, wherever she may sally
Some charming spot to hold her still.
Among her groves and meadows ranging,
Her fondness for them never changing,
She speaks to them as to old friends.
But all too soon the summer ends,
And golden autumn is arriving.
Pale nature shudders, tempest-tossed,
Decked out as for a holocaust . . .
The north wind breathes and bellows, driving
The clouds before him – can it be?
Winter, the sorceress, 'tis she!

In many guises she comes flying:
Upon the oak her tufts are hung;
About the hills and meadows lying,
Her billowy soft rugs are flung;
A touch, and the sharp cliffs are bevelled,
The river and its banks are levelled;
Frost glistens. Mother Winter's arts
Are dazzling, and rejoice our hearts.
But Tanya does not share our pleasure,
And heedless of the winter fun,
She does not sniff the cold, or run
To the low roof to fetch her measure
Of snow, and wash her face and chest.
She glances at the road, distressed.

The day upon which they intended
To leave is gone; they let time slip
Away, while the old sleigh was mended
And re-upholstered for the trip.
The three kibitkas customary
Are loaded with what's necessary;
With chairs, chests, featherbeds they cram
Great casseroles and jars of jam
And fowl in cages (these one slaughters
In town), and pots and pans and gear
Of all sorts; finally you hear
A noise off in the servants' quarters
Of loud farewells and crying maids;
And now they bring out eighteen jades,

And while the breakfast is preparing
They hitch them to the master's sleigh;
Coachmen and wenches vie in swearing;
The loads on the kibitkas sway.
The bearded old postilion's mounted –
His nag has ribs that could be counted.
The servants gather at the gates
For the good-byes; the turnout waits.
The ladies enter; now it's gliding
Away, the good old sleigh, at last.
'Farewell, dear haunts that in the past
Were sanctuary, calm, abiding.
Farewell! Is it forever?' cries
Tanya, with overflowing eyes.

Enlightenment may be belated
With us, but grows apace; indeed,
Philosophers have calculated
Five centuries are all we need
To have our roads expertly mended,
And the improvement will be splendid!
For all through Russia there will run
Highways to make the country one.
We shall have arched, cast-iron bridges
And tunnels under water, too,
And if that's not enough to do,
We'll move apart the mountain ridges,
And not a station will be known
Without a tavern of its own.

Just now our roads are bad for coaches;
Forgotten bridges rot and sink;
And at the stations lice and roaches
Refuse to let you sleep a wink;
There are no inns. In a cold cottage
You scarce can get a bowl of pottage:
The menu hangs there, in plain sight,
Merely to tease your appetite;
The while, his clumsy hammer plying,
The rustic Cyclops in the murk
Mends Europe's dainty handiwork,
And blesses, as he is defying,
The ruts and ditches that abound
Wherever there is Russian ground.

A winter journey always finds you
As happy as the day is long.
The smoothness of the road reminds you
Of verses in a hackneyed song.
Our charioteers are spruce and sprightly,
Our tireless troikas sweep on lightly,
Mile-posts rejoice the idle eye,
They look like pickets flashing by.
But Tanya's mother, not ignoring
The cost of post horses, was glad
To use her own, and hence they had
To rest the nags; the halts were boring,
And Tanya found the journey bleak.
They had to travel for a week.

The goal is there before them. Blazing
Like fire, the golden crosses soar
Where cupolas their heads are raising
Above white Moscow as of yore.
Ah, friends, how I rejoiced, beholding
The panoramic view unfolding
Of park and palace, spire and dome,
The scenes that call the rover home.
How often, sick with separation,
In far-off places, strange and new,
My thoughts, oh, Moscow, turned to you,
And you filled my imagination . . .
Moscow: those syllables can start
A tumult in the Russian heart!

There the Petrovsky Palace, hiding
Its splendour among ancient trees,
Stands grim and grand, morosely priding
Itself upon its memories.
For here, Napoleon, elated
With his last victory, awaited
In vain a Moscow on her knees
To tender him the Kremlin keys.
But it was not capitulation
My Moscow offered Bonaparte –
No feast, no gift to warm his heart:
But she prepared a conflagration.
From here he watched with thoughtful eyes
The fierce flames reddening the skies.

You, witness of that fallen glory,
Farewell, proud palace! But why wait?
On with the journey and the story!
The columns of the city gate
Gleam white; the sleigh, more swift than steady,
Bumps down Tverskaya Street already.
Past sentry boxes now they fly,
Shops, lamp posts, mansions, huts flash by,
Parks, kitchen gardens, monasteries,
Sleighs, pharmacies and boulevards,
Cossacks, Bokharans, merchants, Guards,
Peasants, and boys with cheeks like cherries,
Lions on gates with stony jaws,
And crosses black with flocks of daws.

39–40

So to their destination straightway
They travelled, but a dull hour passed
Before they halted at a gateway
Off in a narrow lane, at last.
They'd come to an old aunt, now failing –
For four long years she had been ailing.
A Kalmuck, spectacled and worn,
Flings wide the door; his caftan's torn,
He holds a stocking he was mending;
Upon the parlour sofa lies
The princess, and her feeble cries
Of welcome are indeed heart-rending.
The two old women weep, embrace,
And soon their tongues begin to race.

'*Princesse!*' 'Pachette! I can't believe it!'
'Yes, after all these years, Aline!'
'How long do you remain?' 'Conceive it!'
'Sit down, *mon ange*!' 'My dear *Cousine*!'
'It's like a novel . . . life's so chancey . . .'
'And this is my Tatyana.' 'Fancy!
Come here, my dear. Why, this seems all
A dream . . . *Cousine*, do you recall
Your Grandison?' 'I can't remember –
My Grandison? Oh, Grandison!
Where is he? Yes, I know the one.'
'He lives in Moscow. Last December
It was he came to visit me.
His son was married recently.

'The other . . . But we've time tomorrow,
N'*est-ce pas*, for all we want of talk?
We'll show off Tanya. To my sorrow,
I can't go out: I cannot walk –
My legs betray me . . . But it's tiring
To travel, you must be desiring
As I am, too, a little rest:
We'll go together . . . Oh, my chest! . . .
Just think, this joy, I can't endure it,
Let alone grief . . . I have no strength . . .
My dear, when old age comes at length
It's misery, and who can cure it?'
At that she could no longer hide
Her weakness, and she coughed and cried.

Tatyana cannot but be grateful
To the kind invalid, and yet
She finds the city cold and hateful,
And does not cease to pine and fret.
Behind the strange bed's silken curtain
She lies for hours, with sleep uncertain;
And the poor girl is roused betimes
Each morning by the Moscow chimes,
The call to early labours dinning;
Out of the window she may stare –
She will not find her meadows there,
When the deep shades of night are thinning:
She sees a court she does not know,
A kitchen and a fence below.

There is a dinner-party daily
Where Tanya's met with 'oh-s' and 'ah-s,'
Her wistful languor greeted gaily
By grandmammas and grandpapas.
The relatives – and there are dozens –
Are cordial to the country cousins,
And all exclaim delightedly
And offer hospitality.
'How Tanya's grown! Why, how long is it
Since you were christened? Gracious sakes!
I boxed your ears! I gave you cakes!'
She hears it all at every visit.
In chorus the old ladies cry:
'Dear me, the years have just flown by!'

45

They do not change, depend upon it,
But keep to their familiar ways:
Princess Yelena wears the bonnet
Of tulle she wore in other days;
Lukerya Lvovna still paints thickly,
Lubov Petrovna lies as quickly,
Ivan Petrovich ne'er was keen,
Semyon Petrovich is as mean,
Aunt Pelageya still possesses
Monsieur Finemouche, friend of the house,
And the same pom, and the same spouse,
The well-known clubman, who, God bless us,
Is just as deaf and just as meek,
And gorges seven days a week.

46

Their daughters, after due embraces,
Examine Tanya silently
From head to foot, and Moscow's Graces
Are quite perplexed by such as she;
They find her odd, a bit affected,
Provincial, as might be expected,
And namby-pamby, colourless
And thin, but pretty, they confess.
Yet soon they give up their pretences,
Invite her, kiss her, press her hands,
Fluff up her hair as style commands,
And murmur singsong confidences,
Relating with more zest than art
The girlish secrets of the heart.

Reciting all their hopes with candour,
Their conquests and their pranks with glee;
Embellished with a little slander,
The guileless talk flows readily.
Then they demand in compensation
That she engage in a narration
Of her own heart's shy hopes and fears;
But Tanya, dreaming, scarcely hears,
And does not pay the least attention,
But listens with an absent smile,
And guards in silence all the while
The secret she will never mention,
The treasure none can ever guess,
The source of tears and happiness.

The parlour hums with conversation,
In which Tatyana ought to share,
She thinks, but it is sheer vexation
To hear the vulgar chatter there.
Such people with each day grow duller,
Their very slander has no colour;
And every query, every tale,
Their news, their gossip – all are stale.
The hours go by: they do not waken;
No witty thought occurs, no word
Even by accident is heard
Whereby the mind or heart is shaken.
Oh, empty world! Oh, stupid folk
Who neither crack nor are a joke!

Viewed by the archive youths who cluster
At any gathering or dance,
The poor young girl does not pass muster –
They eye our heroine askance.
One clownish fellow, idly leaning
Against a door, remarks with meaning
That she's ideal – he must jot
A poem to her on the spot.
Once Vyazemsky sat down beside her
When he was calling on an aunt
Where entertainment was but scant;
And an old gentleman espied her,
Asked who she was, set straight his wig,
And gave his neighbour's ribs a dig.

But where Melpomene's bold gesture
Displays to the indifferent crowd
The tawdry glitter of her vesture,
The while she howls both long and loud;
Where Thalia as she's gently napping
Is heedless of the friendly clapping;
And where the youthful galaxy
Admires alone Terpsichore
(As was the case, upon my honour,
In our time too, in days of old),
The proud lorgnettes the ladies hold
Were in no instance trained upon her,
Nor, from the loge and the parterre,
The eyeglass of the connoisseur.

They take her to the Club for dances.
The rooms are thronged and hot and gay.
The blare, the lights, the shining glances,
The couples as they whirl away,
The lovely ladies' filmy dresses,
The balcony where such a press is,
The young and hopeful brides-to-be,
Confound the senses suddenly.
Here dandies now in the ascendant
Show off their impudence, their vests,
Their monocles that rake the guests.
And here hussars on leave, resplendent
And thunderous, flock eagerly:
They come, they conquer, and they flee.

The stars of night are fair and many,
The Moscow belles are many, too.
Yet brighter shines the moon than any
Of her companions in the blue.
But she in whom my thoughts are rooted,
Before whom my bold lyre is muted,
'Mid maids and matrons seems to glide
Like to the moon in lonely pride.
How heavenly, as she advances,
Her motion, in pure splendour dressed!
What languor fills her lovely breast!
What languor in her magic glances!
But now, enough, have done; for you
Have paid to folly what's her due.

53

They waltz, they bow, they curtsey, flitting
About: a noisy laughing host . . .
While unobserved, Tatyana's sitting
Between two aunts, beside a post,
And stares unseeing, in no hurry
To join the hateful worldly flurry.
She stifles here . . . her heart is sore,
And turns to what is hers no more:
The country life, the rustic hovels,
The lonely thicket where a stream
Is all abubble and agleam,
Her flowers, her romantic novels,
And most, the linden-shaded ways
Where *he* had met her ravished gaze.

54

Thus far away her thoughts are flying;
The world, the ball, are both forgot,
When a great general, espying
The girl, stands rooted to the spot.
The aunts, of one thing only thinking,
Each to the other slyly winking,
Together nudge Tatyana and
Each whispers from behind her hand:
'Look quickly to the left.' But balking,
She asks: 'The left? What's there to see?'
'Just look . . . that man . . . he's one of three
In uniform . . . Now he is walking
Away, his profile may be seen . . .'
'Who? That fat general, you mean?'

Tatyana's brilliant catch discerning,
We think good wishes are the thing.
But it is time I was returning
To him of whom indeed I sing . . .
And by the way, now that I mention
The subject, give me your attention.
Of my young friend I sing, and all
His whims; O epic Muse, let fall
Thy blessing on my task; thy beauty
Pray lend my verse. Upon my way
Be thou my staff, nor let me stray.
Enough. Though late, I've done my duty,
To classicism doffed my hat.
Here's the exordium. That's that!

CHAPTER EIGHT

Fare thee well! and if for ever,
Still for ever, fare thee well.
BYRON

I

When a Lyceum lad, I flourished,
And roamed its gardens at my ease,
On Apuleius gladly nourished,
While Cicero could scarcely please;
When in the springtime I would dally
To watch the swans in some dim valley
And hear, above the lake, their cries,
The Muse first shone before my eyes.
My student cell grew bright with treasures
Such as the Muse alone can bring;
Thither she came to sport and sing
Of youthful pranks and childish pleasures.
And of the glorious days of old,
Of all the dreams the heart can hold.

[186]

And the world smiled upon her, pressing
On us the favours that men crave;
We won good old Derzhavin's blessing
Upon the threshold of his grave.

....
....
....
....
....,....
....
....
....
....
....

And I, all discipline refusing,
Took wilful passion for my guide;
My path was what the crowd was choosing;
The lively Muse was at my side
At giddy feasts and wild discussions,
And when, at midnight, madcap Russians,
We scared patrols with blatant noise;
She shared our banquets, crowned our joys –
Like a Bacchante at the revels,
Sang for the guests across the wine,
And ardently this Muse of mine
Was wooed by passionate young devils.
My flighty friend made quite a stir,
In short, and I was proud of her.

But this gay circle I deserted,
And fled afar . . . She followed me.
How often, by her tales diverted
As I fared onward gloomily,
I heard her friendly accents soften;
And on Caucasian cliffs how often,
Like pale Lenore, by moonlight she
Would gallop side by side with me!
How oft on the dark shores of Tauris
She bade me hear the waters sing,
The Nereids' low murmuring,
The sounding waves' eternal chorus,
And the deep seas His praise rehearse
Who fathered the vast universe.

5

The feasts where wealth and wit were squandered,
The dazzling capital, forgot –
To sad Moldavia she wandered,
And in that far and savage spot
Among the tents of nomads moving,
Full soon my errant Muse was proving
As wild as they: forsook her songs
For the wild steppes' barbaric tongues,
The language of the gods rejected. . . .
Then all is changed. For lo! she veers,
And as a rural miss appears
Within my garden, unexpected;
There, wistful-eyed, behold her stand,
With a French volume in her hand.

And now for the first time I'm bringing
My Muse to a superb soirée;
And jealous fears my heart are stinging
As I her rustic charms survey.
Past close-ranked guests, aristocratic,
Renowned, resplendent, diplomatic,
Fine ladies, military fops,
She glides; and now serenely stops,
And, seated, finds the scene beguiling:
The noisy press so brightly lit,
The sheen of silks, the flash of wit,
The gallants past the hostess filing,
The ladies, each a picture when
Framed sombrely by gentlemen.

She likes the talk of haughty sages
Pursued with so much elegance;
And the assorted ranks and ages,
And pride that ever looks askance.
But in a corner who is standing,
The throng with a mute eye commanding?
He seems, indeed, an alien here,
To whom these faces all appear
But tiresome ghosts. Can we unmask him?
And does his sombre aspect mean
Offended vanity or spleen?
Why is he here? Who is he? Ask him!
Can it be Eugene? Truly? . . . Aye!
'When did he get here, by the by?

8

'Has he grown tame at last, and mellow?
Or does he follow his old bent
And as of yore play the odd fellow?
Pray whom now does he represent?
Would he be Melmoth or Childe Harold,
Or as a Quaker go apparelled,
A bigot seem – a patriot –
A cosmopolitan – or what?
To a new pose will he be goaded,
Or in the end will he just be
A decent chap – like you and me?
I say: give up a style outmoded.
It's time he ceased to be a show . . .'
'Ah, then you know him?' 'Yes, and no.'

9

'Then why upbraid him thus severely?
Is it because we like to sit
Upon the judgement-seat, or merely
Because rash ardour and quick wit
Are found absurd or else offensive
By those whose parts are not extensive?
Is it because intelligence
Loves elbow-room and thrusts us hence?
Or is stupidity malicious –
And trifles of importance to
Important folk, and is it true
That only mediocrity
Befits and pleases you and me?'

Blesséd is he who could be merry
And young in youth; blesséd is he
Who ripened, like good port or sherry,
As years went by, and readily
Grew worldly-wise as life grew chilly,
Gave up his dreams as wild and silly:
At twenty to the fashion bred,
At thirty profitably wed,
Quite free of all his debts at fifty,
Obtaining, with himself to thank,
First glory, and then wealth and rank,
All in good time, serene and thrifty –
Of whom 'twas said throughout his span:
X. is an admirable man.

11

But oh, how deeply we must rue it,
That youth was given us in vain,
That we were hourly faithless to it,
And that it cheated us again;
That our bright pristine hopes grew battered,
Our freshest dreams grew sear, and scattered
Like leaves that in wet autumn stray,
Wind-tossed, and all too soon decay.
It's maddening to see before you
A row of dinners, dull and sure,
Find life a function to endure,
Go with the solemn folk who bore you,
For all their views and passions not,
At heart, giving a single jot.

The gossips ever are malicious,
And it is very hard to bear
When they proclaim you odd or vicious,
Dub you a rogue, which is unfair,
Or else my Demon – condemnation
Enough to kill a reputation.
Onegin (I return to him),
Having, to satisfy a whim,
Dispatched the friend he used to treasure,
And, with no aim on which to fix,
Having attained to twenty-six –
Blasé, grown tired of empty leisure,
Without affairs, or rank, or wife,
Found nothing fit to fill his life.

Thus he grew restless and decided
That he must have a change of scene
(A plaguey wish by which are guided
The few who relish toil and teen).
He left his rustics to their tillage,
Abandoning his pleasant village,
The fields' and forests' solitude
Where still the bloody ghost pursued,
And started on his aimless cruising,
By one emotion only stirred;
Till travel, as you'll have inferred,
Ceased, like all else, to be amusing.
So he returned, took Chatzky's cue,
And forthwith to a ball he flew.

And now the guests, exchanging glances,
And whispering, make quite a stir:
A lady down the room advances,
A haughty general after her.
She is not hurried, is not chilly,
Nor full of idle chat and silly;
She lacks the look of snobbishness,
The cold pretensions to success,
The little tricks that are affected
By ladies in society . . .
Hers is a still simplicity.
She seems the image quite perfected
Of *comme il faut* – Shishkov, berate
Me if you must: I can't translate.

The ladies all pressed closer to her;
Old women smiled as she went by;
Men, while they did not dare pursue her,
Bowed lower, sought to catch her eye;
Young girls, in passing, hushed their chatter;
The general, since such tributes flatter
An escort much, puffed out his chest
And raised his nose above the rest.
She was no beauty: that were fiction
To claim, yet she had not a trace,
From head to foot, in form or face,
Of what, in fashionable diction
And in high London circles, they
Term *vulgar*. To my great dismay,

Although I find it so expressive,
The word is one I can't translate:
Its vogue – since we are not progressive,
And the word's new – cannot be great.
For epigrams it would be splendid . . .
But here's our lady unattended.
All nonchalance and charm and grace,
She at a table took her place
Beside that most superb of creatures,
Fair Nina Voronskaya, who
Presents to the Neva a view
Of Cleopatra, but whose features,
However dazzling to the sight,
Cannot eclipse her neighbour's quite.

'Can it, indeed,' thinks Eugene, 'can it
Be she? It is . . . But no . . . And yet . . .
To come, as from another planet,
From that dull hole . . .' And his lorgnette
Repeatedly and almost grimly
Is trained on her whose features dimly
Remind him of a face forgot.
'Forgive me, Prince, but can you not
Say who it is that now the Spanish
Ambassador is speaking to?
She's wearing raspberry.' 'Yes, you
Have been away! Before you vanish
Again, you'll meet her, 'pon my life!'
'But tell me who she is.' 'My wife.'

'Well, that is news – couldn't be better!
Been married long?' 'Two years.' 'To whom?'
'A Larina.' 'Tanya?' 'You've met her?'
'I am their neighbour.' 'Come, resume
Your friendship.' At this invitation
The prince's comrade and relation
Now met his spouse. The princess gazed
At Eugene . . . If she was amazed,
And if the sudden sight dismayed her,
And if her soul was deeply stirred,
No look, no tremor, not a word
In any small degree betrayed her:
Her manner was what it had been
Before, her bow was as serene.

Not only did she fail to shiver,
Turn pale or blush, as one distressed . . .
Her eyebrows did not even quiver,
Nor yet were her soft lips compressed.
Not all Onegin's observation
Could show him an approximation
To Tanya of the days that were;
He wanted to converse with her
And . . . could not. Now she spoke, inquiring
When he had come, and if, of late,
He'd had a glimpse of his estate;
Then, with a look that showed her tiring,
Begged that her husband suffer her
To leave . . . Our Eugene could not stir.

Can it be that Tatyana truly
Whom, at the start of our romance,
Quite *tête à tête* he'd lectured duly
(You will recall the circumstance)?
How noble was the tone he'd taken;
The spot itself was God-forsaken.
Can this be she who long since wrote –
He has it still – a touching note,
A letter heartfelt, artless, candid;
That little girl . . . is it a dream?
That little girl he did not deem
It wrong to scorn when pride commanded –
Can it be she who only now
Showed him so cold and calm a brow?

He quits the rout, and, meditating,
Drives home; and so at last to bed:
Thoughts sad and sweet still agitating
The sleepless fellow's heart and head.
He wakes to find a note – that's pleasant:
The prince invites him to be present
At a soirée. 'God! to see her! . . .
I'll go!' And he does not defer
The polite 'yes' that is behooving.
Is he bewitched? It's very droll.
By what is his cold, torpid soul
Now stirred? Is it vexation moving
The man? Or vanity, forsooth?
Or love, the grave concern of youth?

He counts the slow hours, vainly trying
To hurry them: he cannot wait.
The clock strikes ten: he's off, he's flying,
And suddenly he's at the gate.
He goes in to the princess, quaking;
Tatyana is alone; but making
An effort to converse with her,
He finds that no remarks occur
To him; and thereby sadly daunted,
Onegin fumbles as he seeks
To answer when the lady speaks.
By one persistent thought he's haunted.
He does not cease his stubborn stare:
She sits with an untroubled air.

The husband enters: the appalling
Bleak *tête à tête* concludes; he cheers
His friend Onegin by recalling
The pranks and jokes of former years.
The guests, arriving, hear their laughter.
The talk is seasoned well thereafter
With the coarse salt of malice, while
Light nothings, spoken without guile
And without foolish affectation,
Give way in turn to common sense:
Not deep or learned or intense,
But reasonable conversation,
That does not frighten anyone
With a too wanton kind of fun.

Here the patricians congregated,
Here fashionables would repair,
The dolts that must be tolerated,
The faces one meets everywhere;
Here, bonneted and wearing roses,
And with the malice time imposes,
Were ladies of a certain age,
And prim young misses looking sage;
Here an ambassador was weighing
Affairs of state, and over there
An ancient, with perfumed grey hair,
Was jesting subtly and displaying
The fine keen wit of yesteryear
Which nowadays seems somewhat queer.

Here was a man who liked to scatter
Neat epigrams, and was annoyed
By tea too sweet, the ladies' chatter,
The tone the gentlemen employed,
Poor novels that won approbation,
Two sisters' royal decoration,
The lies that journals perpetrate,
The war, the snow-fall, and his mate.
....
....
....
....
....
....

And here too was [Prolasov], stunted
In soul, of all the guests the least
Admired – in sketching whom you blunted
Your wicked pencils, oh, St Priest!
While in the doorway took his station –
As perfect as an illustration –
A ballroom tyrant, tightly laced,
Mute, motionless, and cherub-faced;
And there a traveller from a distance,
A brazen fellow, starched and proud,
With studied ways amused the crowd
That scarce had heard of his existence,
And though he met with no rebuff,
The guests' sly glances were enough.

But Eugene's sole preoccupation
Was with Tatyana – not, forsooth,
The poor shy girl whose adoration
Of him had filled her simple youth,
But the proud princess, cold and serious,
The queen, aloof, remote, imperious,
Of the magnificent Neva.
Oh, humans, like your first mamma,
Ancestral Eve, you find delightful
Not what you have, but what you see
Afar: the serpent and the tree
Seduce you, though the cost be frightful.
Forbidden fruits alone entice –
Without them, there's no paradise.

How changed Tatyana is! How truly
She knows her role! With none to thank –
Tutored by her own wit – she duly
Bears the proud burden of her rank!
Who, in this cool majestic woman,
The ballroom's ruler, scarcely human,
Would dare to seek that gentle girl?
And he had set her heart awhirl!
When nights were dark and she, forsaken
By Morpheus, her dark eyes would rest
Upon the moon, and her young breast
By virginal desires was shaken,
Then in a dream that naught could dim
She'd walk life's humble road with him.

To love all ages owe submission;
To youthful hearts its tempests bring
The very boon they would petition,
As fields are blest by storms of spring:
The rain of passion is not cruel,
But bears refreshment and renewal –
There is a quickening at the root
That bodes full flowers and honeyed fruit.
But at the late and sterile season,
At the sad turning of the years,
The tread of passion augurs tears:
Thus autumn gusts deal death and treason,
And turn the meadow to a marsh
And leave the forests gaunt and harsh.

Alas, our poor Onegin's smitten:
Tatyana fills his every thought;
His heart is by such anguish bitten
As only passion can have wrought.
He does not heed the mind's reproaches,
But, rain or shine, each day his coach is
Before her door; he waits for her;
No shadow could be faithfuller.
He knows delight when he's adjusting
The boa on her shoulders, and
When his hot fingers touch her hand,
Or when through liveried throngs he's thrusting
A way for her; he's happy if
He may pick up her handkerchief.

She does not heed; and sore it grieves him
To note how little she is stirred;
With perfect freedom she receives him;
When guests are there, she says a word
Or bows to him – a cold convention;
At times she pays him no attention;
She has no trace of coquetry –
It's frowned on in society.
But though Onegin's peace forsake him
And his cheek pale, she does not see
Or does not care; and all agree
Consumption yet may overtake him.
He's sent to doctors, the Neva's
Best leeches send him to the spas.

But he refuses; he's preparing
To meet his fathers speedily;
Tatyana shows no sign of caring
(Such is the sex, you will agree);
And he, reluctant to surrender,
Still clings to hope, though it be slender,
And far too wretched to be meek
He pens, with trembling hand and weak,
A missive eloquent of passion.
He did not value letters much,
And rightly, but his pain was such
That write he must, and in this fashion –
Perhaps 'twill please you if I quote
The very words Onegin wrote.

All is foreseen: when I confess
My mournful secret you will shun me:
And the grave eyes that have undone me
Will look with scorn on my distress!
Indeed what can I hope for, after
You know the truth? What is the use
Of speech? For what malicious laughter
Do I thus give you an excuse?

We met by chance; I, though perceiving
Affection's spark in you, believing
Myself mistaken, did not dare
To let the tender habit seize me;
Although my freedom did not please me,
The loss of it I could not bear.
And one thing more put us asunder –
Poor Lensky fell . . . that luckless day,
From all the heart holds dear, my blunder
Forced me to tear my heart away;
An alien, roving unrestricted,
I took this peace, this liberty,
For happiness. Good God! I see
How justly now I am afflicted.

No, to be with you constantly;
To follow you with deep devotion;
And with enamoured eyes to see
Each smile of yours, each glance, each motion;
To listen to you, late and soon;
To know you: spirit tuned to spirit;
In torment at your feet to swoon –
Were bliss; and death? I should not fear it!

It may not be: without relief,
I drag myself about; time's hasting,
And it is precious, being brief:
Yet in vain boredom I am wasting
The hours allotted me by Fate,
And oh, they are a weary weight!
My days are counted: I've had warning;
But to endure I need one boon –
I must be certain in the morning
Of seeing you by afternoon. . . .

I fear lest in my supplication
You should perceive with eye severe
A trick worthy of detestation;
Already your reproach I hear.
If you but knew how agonizing
It is to parch with hot desire,
By mental effort tranquillizing
The blood that burns with frantic fire;
To long to clasp your knees, and, throbbing
With anguish, pour forth at your feet
Appeal, complaint, confession, sobbing
The wretched story out, complete, –
And longing thus, be forced to meet you
With a feigned chill in look and voice,
Converse at ease, seem to rejoice,
And with a cheerful eye to greet you! –

So be it; on your word I wait;
I could not choose but speak, I'm guided
Now by your will; my lot's decided;
And I surrender to my fate.

There is no answer to his letter;
A second, and a third he sends,
Alas, these missives fare no better.
Then, at a party he attends
He comes upon her, as he enters.
How firmly her attention centres
On all but him! She never sees
Onegin, but she seems to freeze
As he comes near; it's no illusion:
Incensed, she seals her lips, while he
Can only watch her fixedly.
Where is compassion, where confusion?
Is there a sign of tears? No trace!
Mute anger only marks her face . . .

Yes, and the fear of the impression
The world would gain if it should learn
About her early indiscretion . . .
No more my Eugene could discern.
All hope is gone! He leaves, and curses
His madness – and again immerses
Himself so deep in it that he
Once more forsakes society.
Now in his study he bethought him
Of days long past, when he had been
A giddy fop, and cruel spleen
Had chased him and had quickly caught him,
And locked him in a corner where
The lonely gloom was hard to bear.

Again a book was his sole crony –
He read at will: Gibbon, Rousseau,
Chamfort and Herder and Manzoni,
Madame de Staël, Bichat, Tissot;
Devoured Bayle, the arrant sceptic,
And Fontenelle, acute, eupeptic;
And Russians too he would peruse:
He was not one to pick and choose.
He read miscellany and journal,
The magazines that like to scold
Us all, and where I now am told
That my performance is infernal,
Though once they praised my magic pen:
E sempre bene, gentlemen.

What of it? Though his eyes were busy,
His mind was ever far away;
With whirling thoughts his soul grew dizzy,
And dreams and musings far from gay.
The page he read could scarcely bore him,
Because, between the lines before him,
Another set of lines transpired
Of which Onegin never tired.
These were the secret fond traditions
Of intimacies of the past,
And rootless dreams that could not last,
Vague threats, predictions, and suspicions,
A fairy tale that lasts the night,
Or letters that a girl might write.

And as he reads, both thought and feeling
Are lulled to sleep, and readily
Imagination is unreeling
Its parti-coloured pageantry.
The first clear picture is disclosing
A youth, who on the snow seems dozing;
As Eugene stares his heart is chilled
To hear a voice cry: 'Well? He's killed.'
He sees forgotten foes, malicious
Detractors, cowardly and vile,
And cruel traitresses who smile,
And old companions, dull and vicious;
A country house he next may see –
She's at the window – always she! . . .

Thus sunk in reveries, he nearly
Went raving mad or worse: became
A poet – this were paying dearly
For dreams, and would have been a shame.
But by some influence despotic,
Call it magnetic or hypnotic,
My brainless pupil almost learned
The way a Russian verse is turned.
He looked the poet, when he'd let a
Long evening pass, while he would sit
Beside the fire and hum to it
'*Idol mio*' or '*Benedetta*',
Until the flames blazed up anew
Fed by his slipper or review.

The days speed by; before you know it
New warmth has melted winter's chain;
But he has not become a poet,
He did not die or go insane.
And now, at spring's bright invitation,
He quits his place of hibernation –
Close as a marmot would require –
The double windows, the snug fire;
And one fine morning finds him flying
Past the Neva in a swift sleigh;
On the streaked ice the sunbeams play;
Upon the streets the snow is lying,
By thaw and grimy steps defaced.
But whither in such anxious haste

Does Eugene drive? Yes, I suspected
You knew the answer – as you say:
This same odd fellow, uncorrected,
To his Tatyana makes his way.
Looking too corpselike to be nobby,
He walks into the empty lobby.
Each room he finds unoccupied.
Here is a door – he flings it wide,
And halts in sudden deep confusion;
What sight thus fills him with dismay?
The princess, pale, in négligé,
Pores o'er a letter, in seclusion;
Her cheek rests on her hand, and she
Is weeping, weeping quietly.

Her voiceless grief was past disguising;
In that swift moment you could see
The former Tanya, recognizing
Her in the princess readily.
Eugene, like one awaiting sentence,
Fell at her feet in wild repentance;
She shuddered, wordless, yet her eyes
Betrayed no anger, no surprise
As she surveyed him . . . His dejected
And healthless look, his dumb remorse –
These spoke to her with silent force.
And in her soul was resurrected
The simple girl, whose dreams, whose ways,
Whose heart belonged to other days.

She does not raise him, does not falter;
Nor from his greedy lips withdraws
Her nerveless hand; she does not alter
Her fixed regard throughout the pause.
What are her reveries unspoken?
The silence at long last is broken
As she says gently: 'Rise; have done.
I must say candid words or none.
Onegin, need I ask you whether
You still retain the memory
Of that lost hour beneath the tree
When destiny brought us together?
You lectured me, I listened, meek;
Today it is my turn to speak.

'Then I was younger, maybe better,
Onegin, and I loved you; well?
How did you take my girlish letter?
Your heart responded how? Pray, tell!
Most harshly: there was no disguising
Your scorn. You did not find surprising
The plain girl's love? Why, even now,
I freeze – good God! – recalling how
You came and preached at me so brightly –
Your look that made my spirit sink!
But for that sermon do not think
I blame you . . . For you acted rightly,
Indeed, you played a noble role:
I thank you from my inmost soul . . .

'Then, far from Moscow's noise and glitter,
Off in the wilds – is it not true? –
You did not like me . . . That was bitter,
But worse, what now you choose to do!
Why do you pay me these attentions?
Because society's conventions,
Deferring to my wealth and rank,
Have given me prestige? Be frank!
Because my husband's decoration,
A soldier's, wins us friends at Court,
And all would relish the report
That I had stained my reputation –
'Twould give you in society
A pleasant notoriety?

'I cannot help it: I am weeping. . . .
If you recall your Tanya still,
There is one thought you should be keeping
In mind: if I but had my will,
You'd treat me in the old harsh fashion,
Not offer this insulting passion,
These endless letters and these tears.
My childish dreams, my tender years
Aroused your pity then. . . . You're kneeling
Here at my feet. But dare you say
In truth what brought you here today?
What petty thought, what trivial feeling?
Can you, so generous, so keen,
Be ruled by what is small and mean?

'To me, Onegin, all these splendours,
The tinsel of unwelcome days,
The homage that the great world tenders,
My modish house and my soirées –
To me all this is naught. This minute
I'd give my house and all that's in it,
This dizzy whirl in fancy-dress,
For a few books, a wilderness
Of flowers, for our modest dwelling,
The scene where first I saw your face,
Onegin, that familiar place,
And for the simple churchyard, telling
Its tale of humble lives, where now
My poor nurse sleeps beneath the bough . . .

'And happiness, before it glided
Away forever, was so near! . . . .
But now my fate is quite decided.
I was in too much haste, I fear;
My mother coaxed and wept; the sequel
You know; besides, all lots were equal
To hapless Tanya . . . Well, and so
I married. Now, I beg you, go.
I know your heart; I need not tremble,
Because your honour and your pride
Must in this matter be your guide.
I love you (why should I dissemble?)
But I became another's wife;
I shall be true to him through life.'

She left him.   There Eugene, forsaken,
Stood thunderstruck. He could not stir.
By what a storm his heart was shaken,
What pride, what grief, what thoughts of her!
But is it spurs that he is hearing?
Tatyana's husband is appearing.
At this unhappy moment we
Must leave my hero; it will be
For a long time . . . Indeed, forever.
Together we have travelled far.
Congratulations! Now we are
Ashore at last, and our endeavour
Is at an end. Hurrah, three cheers!
You'll grant it's time to part, my dears.

Kind reader, I would beg you, whether
You are ally or enemy,
Since we no longer fare together,
To take a friendly leave of me.
Whatever in these careless verses
You seek: say, what the heart rehearses
Of the wild past, or welcome rest,
A living picture, or a jest,
Or merely some mistakes in grammar,
God grant you find some trifle here
To earn a smile, a dream, a tear,
Or cause a journalistic clamour.
And now that I've no more to tell,
I take my leave of you – farewell!

Farewell, strange friend, our journey's ended,
Farewell, my fair ideal, too,
And you whose growth I briskly tended:
My little book. With you I knew
The poet's need (bar inspiration):
The joys of genial conversation,
Oblivion of the world's rough ways.
How many, many flitting days
Have passed since in a hazy vision
I first saw Tanya, dreamy-eyed,
With her Onegin at her side –
Before the crystal with precision
Had shown to my enchanted glance
The vista of a free romance!

But those good friends who were insistent
That the first strophes should be read
To them ... Alas, now some are distant,
Some are no more, as Saadi said.
Onegin's portrait is completed,
But not by them will it be greeted;
And she who for Tatyana posed ...
How many chapters Fate has closed!
Blessed is he who leaves the glory
Of life's gay feast ere time is up,
Who does not drain the brimming cup,
Nor reads the ending of the story,
But drops it without more ado,
As, my Onegin, I drop you.

The last chapter of *Eugene Onegin* was published separately, with the following Foreword (by the author):

'The omitted stanzas have repeatedly given occasion to reproaches and to gibes (which were, however, very just and witty). The author frankly confesses that he had left out of his novel an entire chapter, which described Onegin's travels in Russia. It was for him to indicate the omitted chapter by dots or a numeral; but, to avoid gossip, he decided to number the last chapter of *Eugene Onegin* 'eight' instead of 'nine,' and to sacrifice one of the final stanzas:

> 'Tis time: my pen wants rest from driving:
> I've finished cantos nine, no more;
> With the ninth wave the ship's arriving
> In triumph at the joyous shore;
> And so all hail to you, nine Muses...

'P. A. Katenin (who is not prevented by his admirable poetic talent from being a fine critic) has .

pointed out to us that the omission, though perhaps advantageous to readers, nevertheless injures the plan of the whole composition; for, as a result, the transition from Tatyana, the provincial miss, to Tatyana, the society lady, is unexplained and too sudden. An observation betokening an experienced artist. The author himself felt the justice of it, but he had resolved to omit this chapter for reasons important to him, not to the public. Some fragments of it have been printed; we are reproducing them here, adding several stanzas to them.'

EUGENE ONEGIN GOES
FROM MOSCOW TO NIZHNI-NOVGOROD:

                    . . . and there
Before him, loud with seething traffic,
Lies spread the famous annual fair.

Europe has spurious wines to offer;
The Hindu – diamonds in his coffer;
Here too the plainsman comes and brags,
Hoping to sell his worthless nags;
The sharks who feed on gamblers' passions
Have cards and dice; and not for naught
The landed gentleman has brought
Ripe daughters, dressed in last year's fashions.
All hustle, bustle, tell great lies,
And show commercial enterprise.

How dismal!

ONEGIN TRAVELS TO ASTRAKHAN,
AND FROM THERE TO THE CAUCASUS:

He sees the self-willed Terek flinging
Its waves on shores that rise up sheer;
Ahead, a royal eagle winging;
With lowered horns, a lonely deer;
In the steep shade a camel lying;
There a Circassian's horse goes flying;
While round the tents that nomads raise
The Kalmucks' flocks, contented, graze.
Beyond, the Caucasus' tall masses,
A barrier that is no more,
A frontier shattered by the war
That riots through the mountain passes;
And Kura's and Aragva's banks
Behold the Russian tents in ranks.

Beshtau, the sharp-peaked, the eternal
Custodian of the desert, fills
The background, and Mashuk, the vernal,
Towers above the craggy hills,
Mashuk, most health-giving of mountains;
About its magic healing fountains,
A pallid swarm, the patients pour:
Some, honour's victims, scarred by war,
Some, prey to piles, or Aphrodite;
The weak would mend life's fraying thread;
The insults time heaps on her head
Are here cast off, or so the flighty
Coquette believes; the old man dreams
Of youth renewed beside these streams.

Absorbed in bitter meditation
Amidst this dreary family,
Onegin's wistful observation
Rests on the smoky streams, and he
Thinks sadly: 'Why am I not ailing,
Say, from a bullet-wound? Or failing,
Like this decrepit publican?
Why not, like that poor Tula man,
The old assessor, paralytic?
Why don't I travel with a crutch,
Or in the shoulder feel a touch
At least of some complaint arthritic?
How dismal to be sturdy, Lord,
How dismal to be young, and bored!'

THEN ONEGIN VISITS TAURIS:

A land imagination hallows:
Orestes vied there with his friend,
There Mithridates sought his end,
And there beside the rocky shallows
Inspired Mickiewicz used to stand
And dream about his native land.

Ah, you are lovely, shores of Tauris,
From shipboard looming on the sight
As first I saw you there before us
At dawn, by Cytherea's light.
You shone as with a nuptial splendour:
Upon the azure, pale and tender,
The masses of your mountains gleamed,
And valleys, trees, and hamlets seemed

A pattern spread; and soon what yearning
Possessed me, underneath your spell,
Among the huts where Tartars dwell . . .
How ardently this breast was burning!
What anguished longing held me fast!
But, Muse, you must forget the past.

Forget the feelings that held riot
Within me – they have found surcease:
I am an altered man and quiet.
Ye vanished tumults, rest in peace!
Then I required, as I protested,
Vast wastes, and billows diamond-crested,
Steep cliffs above the ocean's purl,
The vision of a haughty girl,
Strange woes that left me broken-hearted . . .
With other days come other dreams,
And with my vanished spring, it seems,
My high-flown fancies have departed.
By now the wine of poesy
Has been diluted heavily.

Now different scenes delight my senses:
A gentle sandy slope will please,
A wicket-gate and broken fences,
A cottage with two rowan trees,
Grey skies, and heaps of straw in billows
Before the threshing-floor, thick willows
Whose shade across the mill-pond lies
That forms the ducklings' paradise.
A balalaika gives me pleasure,
And at the tavern-door the clack

And drunken stamp of the *trepak*,
A housewife seems a perfect treasure!
I want my peace, my pot of *stchi*,
And my own man I want to be.

The other day in rainy weather
I strolled into the farmyard – faugh!
What prosy rubbish altogether,
Stuff that the Flemish school would draw.
In youth, were such the joys I'd count on?
Reply, Bakhchi-Sarai's sad fountain!
Pray, did your ceaseless clamour start
Such feelings in this troubled heart,
When mutely on your brink I pondered
Upon Zarema? To the same
Rich empty rooms Onegin came
When I was gone three years, and wandered
Among those regions drearily,
And thought, I do not doubt, of me.

Odessa was my home then, shrouded
In dust . . . But there the skies are bright;
With sails and rich thick traffic crowded,
The harbour is a busy sight;
The city breathes of Europe; hotly,
On scenes both various and motley,
Shines the resplendent southern sun –
On everything and everyone:
You hear amid the gay street's fluster
The golden tongue Italians speak;
Armenian, Spaniard, Frenchman, Greek,
Proud Slav and stout Moldavian muster;

And strolling with the throng you'll view
Egypt's retired corsair too.

Tumansky in sonorous stanzas
Described the town; we must admit,
When writing his extravaganzas
He turned a partial eye on it.
Lorgnette in hand, our friend would wander,
A veritable poet, yonder,
Alone along the sea-shore; then
He'd take his fascinating pen
And praise Odessa's gardens greatly.
That's fine, but if the truth were told,
Bare steppe is all you will behold;
Just here and there hard labour lately
Compelled young boughs, in sultry heat,
To cast forced shade upon the street.

But where is my disjointed story?
I called Odessa dusty – I
Don't aim to cover it with glory:
To call it dirty is no lie.
Storm-giver Zeus decrees Odessa
For six weeks yearly be a mess, a
Town that's delivered to the flood,
Drenched, deluged, choked with vicious mud;
Immersed in it the houses founder;
On stilts the bold pedestrian
Wades through the streets, if he but can;
Both carriages and people flounder,
The ox with lowered horns must drag
The cab, to spare the feeble nag.

But now the heavy hammer's pounding
Away already: without fail,
The city soon will wear resounding
Hard pavements, like a coat of mail.
And yet Odessa, our wet city,
Wants one thing further, more's the pity;
What is it? Water! And this lack
Means labour fit to break the back . . .
No matter. Why should we be asking
For such a trifle? Why repine
When there's no duty on the wine?
The sea, the southern sun for basking . . .
What more, my friends, do you demand?
Truly, a beatific land.

No sooner did the cannon, sounding
From shipboard, thunder dawn, than I,
Abruptly down the incline bounding,
To the inviting sea would fly.
And then, refreshed after a dipping,
With pipe alight you'd find me sipping
Thick coffee Orientals prize:
A Moslem in his paradise.
I take a stroll. Now cups are clinking
At the casino cosily;
The marker on the balcony
Appears, his broom in hand, still blinking;
Below, though it is early yet,
Two merchants have already met.

The square grows lively now and dizzy
With motley figures: people dart

About, some idle and some busy,
But business holds the greater part.
The child of shrewdness and of daring,
The merchant, to the port is faring
To scan the flags and see what sails
Announce the coming of his bales.
Have they arrived? His calculations
Were set upon those casks of wine.
What shipments are in quarantine?
Have there been any conflagrations?
What talk of famine, plague, or war?
Such is the news he's eager for.

We careless fellows leave the fretting
To merchants; we have but one fear:
The load of oysters they were getting
From Istanbul may not be here.
The oysters? They have come! In rapture
Forth rushes greedy youth to capture
Those fleshy anchorites alive
And gulp them down as they arrive,
Just for a dash of lemon waiting.
Noise, chatter, on the table shine
Bottles of cellar-cooled light wine:
Oton is so accommodating.
The flying hours no one counts,
The fearful bill, unheeded, mounts.

But now the blue of evening darkens,
The opera summons – in a word,
The Orpheus to whom Europe hearkens,
Her pet, Rossini, must be heard.

Let critics carp, he will not grovel:
Always the same and always novel,
He pours out fluent melodies;
They glow, they burn, the ecstasies
They rouse are those of youthful kisses,
The languor and the flame of love
Are in them, and the sparkle of
Aÿ, when, foaming gold, it hisses . . .
But, gentlemen, you may decline
To liken do-re-mi to wine.

Is it the music's fascination
Alone? What of the eye-glass, eh?
Behind the scenes, the assignation?
The prima donna? The ballet?
The box, where, regnant in her splendour,
The merchant's wife, so young and slender,
Displays her languor and her pride
To crowding slaves on every side?
She hears and does not hear the closing
Smooth aria, the eager plea,
The jesting mixed with flattery . . .
Her husband, in the corner, dozing,
Shouts *fora!* in his sleep, and then
He yawns and starts to snore again.

The loud finale sounds, and pushing,
With noisy haste the throng decamps;
Into the square the crowd is rushing,
Beneath the light of stars and lamps.
Ausonia's happy sons are trilling
A merry tune that, all unwilling,

They learned, and we, before we leave,
Are roaring the recitative.
It's late. Odessa sleeps, unruffled;
No breath disturbs the warm still night.
The moon has risen; in a light
Transparent veil the sky is muffled.
No sound, save for the soft slow roar
Of the Black Sea upon the shore.

And so, my home was then Odessa ...

READ MORE IN PENGUIN

In every corner of the world, on every subject under the sun, Penguin represents quality and variety – the very best in publishing today.

For complete information about books available from Penguin – including Puffins, Penguin Classics and Arkana – and how to order them, write to us at the appropriate address below. Please note that for copyright reasons the selection of books varies from country to country.

In the United Kingdom: Please write to *Dept. EP, Penguin Books Ltd, Bath Road, Harmondsworth, West Drayton, Middlesex UB7 0DA*

In the United States: Please write to *Consumer Sales, Penguin Putnam Inc., P.O. Box 12289 Dept. B, Newark, New Jersey 07101-5289.* VISA and MasterCard holders call 1-800-788-6262 to order Penguin titles

In Canada: Please write to *Penguin Books Canada Ltd, 10 Alcorn Avenue, Suite 300, Toronto, Ontario M4V 3B2*

In Australia: Please write to *Penguin Books Australia Ltd, P.O. Box 257, Ringwood, Victoria 3134*

In New Zealand: Please write to *Penguin Books (NZ) Ltd, Private Bag 102902, North Shore Mail Centre, Auckland 10*

In India: Please write to *Penguin Books India Pvt Ltd, 11 Community Centre, Panchsheel Park, New Delhi 110017*

In the Netherlands: Please write to *Penguin Books Netherlands bv, Postbus 3507, NL-1001 AH Amsterdam*

In Germany: Please write to *Penguin Books Deutschland GmbH, Metzlerstrasse 26, 60594 Frankfurt am Main*

In Spain: Please write to *Penguin Books S. A., Bravo Murillo 19, 1° B, 28015 Madrid*

In Italy: Please write to *Penguin Italia s.r.l., Via Benedetto Croce 2, 20094 Corsico, Milano*

In France: Please write to *Penguin France, Le Carré Wilson, 62 rue Benjamin Baillaud, 31500 Toulouse*

In Japan: Please write to *Penguin Books Japan Ltd, Kaneko Building, 2-3-25 Koraku, Bunkyo-Ku, Tokyo 112*

In South Africa: Please write to *Penguin Books South Africa (Pty) Ltd, Private Bag X14, Parkview, 2122 Johannesburg*

READ MORE IN PENGUIN

A CHOICE OF CLASSICS

Matthew Arnold	**Selected Prose**
Jane Austen	**Emma**
	Lady Susan/The Watsons/Sanditon
	Mansfield Park
	Northanger Abbey
	Persuasion
	Pride and Prejudice
	Sense and Sensibility
William Barnes	**Selected Poems**
Mary Braddon	**Lady Audley's Secret**
Anne Brontë	**Agnes Grey**
	The Tenant of Wildfell Hall
Charlotte Brontë	**Jane Eyre**
	Juvenilia: 1829–35
	The Professor
	Shirley
	Villette
Emily Brontë	**Complete Poems**
	Wuthering Heights
Samuel Butler	**Erewhon**
	The Way of All Flesh
Lord Byron	**Don Juan**
	Selected Poems
Lewis Carroll	**Alice's Adventures in Wonderland**
	The Hunting of the Snark
Thomas Carlyle	**Selected Writings**
Arthur Hugh Clough	**Selected Poems**
Wilkie Collins	**Armadale**
	The Law and the Lady
	The Moonstone
	No Name
	The Woman in White
Charles Darwin	**The Origin of Species**
	Voyage of the Beagle
Benjamin Disraeli	**Coningsby**
	Sybil

READ MORE IN PENGUIN

A CHOICE OF CLASSICS

Charles Dickens	**American Notes for General Circulation**
	Barnaby Rudge
	Bleak House
	The Christmas Books (in two volumes)
	David Copperfield
	Dombey and Son
	Great Expectations
	Hard Times
	Little Dorrit
	Martin Chuzzlewit
	The Mystery of Edwin Drood
	Nicholas Nickleby
	The Old Curiosity Shop
	Oliver Twist
	Our Mutual Friend
	The Pickwick Papers
	Pictures from Italy
	Selected Journalism 1850–1870
	Selected Short Fiction
	Sketches by Boz
	A Tale of Two Cities
George Eliot	**Adam Bede**
	Daniel Deronda
	Felix Holt
	Middlemarch
	The Mill on the Floss
	Romola
	Scenes of Clerical Life
	Silas Marner
Fanny Fern	**Ruth Hall**
Elizabeth Gaskell	**Cranford/Cousin Phillis**
	The Life of Charlotte Brontë
	Mary Barton
	North and South
	Ruth
	Sylvia's Lovers
	Wives and Daughters

READ MORE IN PENGUIN

A CHOICE OF CLASSICS

Edward Gibbon	**The Decline and Fall of the Roman Empire** (in three volumes)
	Memoirs of My Life
George Gissing	**New Grub Street**
	The Odd Women
William Godwin	**Caleb Williams**
	Concerning Political Justice
Thomas Hardy	**Desperate Remedies**
	The Distracted Preacher and Other Tales
	Far from the Madding Crowd
	Jude the Obscure
	The Hand of Ethelberta
	A Laodicean
	The Mayor of Casterbridge
	A Pair of Blue Eyes
	The Return of the Native
	Selected Poems
	Tess of the d'Urbervilles
	The Trumpet-Major
	Two on a Tower
	Under the Greenwood Tree
	The Well-Beloved
	The Woodlanders
George Lyell	**Principles of Geology**
Lord Macaulay	**The History of England**
Henry Mayhew	**London Labour and the London Poor**
George Meredith	**The Egoist**
	The Ordeal of Richard Feverel
John Stuart Mill	**The Autobiography**
	On Liberty
	Principles of Political Economy
William Morris	**News from Nowhere and Other Writings**
John Henry Newman	**Apologia Pro Vita Sua**
Margaret Oliphant	**Miss Marjoribanks**
Robert Owen	**A New View of Society and Other Writings**
Walter Pater	**Marius the Epicurean**
John Ruskin	**Unto This Last and Other Writings**

READ MORE IN PENGUIN

A CHOICE OF CLASSICS

Walter Scott	**The Antiquary**
	Heart of Mid-Lothian
	Ivanhoe
	Kenilworth
	The Tale of Old Mortality
	Rob Roy
	Waverley
Robert Louis Stevenson	**Kidnapped**
	Dr Jekyll and Mr Hyde and Other Stories
	In the South Seas
	The Master of Ballantrae
	Selected Poems
	Weir of Hermiston
William Makepeace Thackeray	**The History of Henry Esmond**
	The History of Pendennis
	The Newcomes
	Vanity Fair
Anthony Trollope	**Barchester Towers**
	Can You Forgive Her?
	Doctor Thorne
	The Eustace Diamonds
	Framley Parsonage
	He Knew He Was Right
	The Last Chronicle of Barset
	Phineas Finn
	The Prime Minister
	The Small House at Allington
	The Warden
	The Way We Live Now
Oscar Wilde	**Complete Short Fiction**
Mary Wollstonecraft	**A Vindication of the Rights of Woman**
	Mary and **Maria** (includes Mary Shelley's **Matilda**)
Dorothy and William Wordsworth	**Home at Grasmere**

READ MORE IN PENGUIN

A CHOICE OF CLASSICS

Honoré de Balzac	**The Black Sheep**
	César Birotteau
	The Chouáns
	Cousin Bette
	Cousin Pons
	Eugénie Grandet
	A Harlot High and Low
	History of the Thirteen
	Lost Illusions
	A Murky Business
	Old Goriot
	Selected Short Stories
	Ursule Mirouët
	The Wild Ass's Skin
J. A. Brillat-Savarin	**The Physiology of Taste**
Charles Baudelaire	**Baudelaire in English**
	Selected Poems
	Selected Writings on Art and Literature
Pierre Corneille	**The Cid/Cinna/The Theatrical Illusion**
Alphonse Daudet	**Letters from My Windmill**
Denis Diderot	**Jacques the Fatalist**
	The Nun
	Rameau's Nephew/D'Alembert's Dream
	Selected Writings on Art and Literature
Alexandre Dumas	**The Count of Monte Cristo**
	The Three Musketeers
Gustave Flaubert	**Bouvard and Pécuchet**
	Flaubert in Egypt
	Madame Bovary
	Salammbo
	Selected Letters
	Sentimental Education
	The Temptation of St Antony
	Three Tales
Victor Hugo	**Les Misérables**
	Notre-Dame of Paris
Laclos	**Les Liaisons Dangereuses**

READ MORE IN PENGUIN

A CHOICE OF CLASSICS

READ MORE IN PENGUIN

A CHOICE OF CLASSICS

Anton Chekhov	**The Duel and Other Stories**
	The Kiss and Other Stories
	The Fiancée and Other Stories
	Lady with Lapdog and Other Stories
	The Party and Other Stories
	Plays (The Cherry Orchard/Ivanov/The Seagull/Uncle Vania/The Bear/The Proposal/A Jubilee/Three Sisters)
Fyodor Dostoyevsky	**The Brothers Karamazov**
	Crime and Punishment
	The Devils
	The Gambler/Bobok/A Nasty Story
	The House of the Dead
	The Idiot
	Netochka Nezvanova
	The Village of Stepanchikovo
	Notes from Underground/The Double
Nikolai Gogol	**Dead Souls**
	Diary of a Madman and Other Stories
Alexander Pushkin	**Eugene Onegin**
	The Queen of Spades and Other Stories
	Tales of Belkin
Leo Tolstoy	**Anna Karenin**
	Childhood, Boyhood, Youth
	A Confession
	How Much Land Does a Man Need?
	Master and Man and Other Stories
	Resurrection
	The Sebastopol Sketches
	What is Art?
	War and Peace
Ivan Turgenev	**Fathers and Sons**
	First Love
	A Month in the Country
	On the Eve
	Rudin
	Sketches from a Hunter's Album